GLEAMERS CHRONICLE

Winter Shadows

I0777496

Winter Shadows

GLEAMERS CHRONICLE

L. B. ANNE

JOA PRESS
FLORIDA

This is a work of fiction. Names, characters, places, and incidents either are the product of the author's imagination or are used fictitiously. Any resemblance to actual persons, living or dead, events, or locales is entirely coincidental.

Copyright © 2024 by L. B. Anne

All rights reserved

For information, Address JOA Press

P.O. Box 7984, Seminole, Florida 33775.

www.joapress.com

Cover art © 2024 by Anna Spies

Edited by Cristy Watson

All rights reserved.

No part of this publication may be reproduced, distributed, or transmitted in any form or by any means, including photocopying, recording, or other electronic or mechanical methods, without the prior written permission of the publisher, except as permitted by U.S. copyright law.

Unless otherwise indicated, scripture quotations are from the New King James Version Copyright ©1982 by Thomas Nelson, Inc. Used by permission.

Library of Congress Control Number: 2024919724

ISBN 979-8-9889776-4-3

DEDICATION

For all of my Sheena meyer series readers, Thank your for sticking with me on this journey. Alaysia, You are a constant inspiration.

My grandmother once told me that the world was full of things we didn't understand.

"Magical things?" I asked.

"There is no magic, Alaina," she replied. "There is only the gleam."

CHAPTER ONE

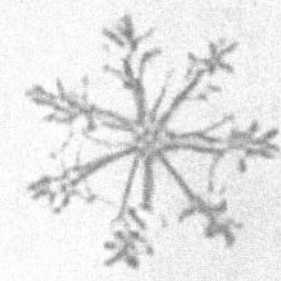

It was the first night of winter break, and no matter how hard I tried, I couldn't fall asleep. I lay in bed, watching snowflakes drift past my window and counting the days until Christmas. There was still almost two weeks to go.

Eventually, as I watched the snowflakes melting against the glass, my eyelids grew heavier, each blink slower than the last. Holiday music played softly from somewhere in the house, and my parents spoke in hushed tones thinking I was already asleep.

Just when I finally felt myself drifting off, a glint of light zipped past my window—fast and bright, cutting through the night.

My eyes snapped open. *What was that?*

I jumped out of bed and pressed my face to the glass, hoping to catch another glimpse as my imagination ran wild with thoughts of fairies and flying unicorns. That magical fantasy world had taken over my mind ever since I'd finished *The Land Before Wishes*, a book I still needed to return to the library. Maybe one of those mythical creatures had ditched the book world and came to life to save me from having to go to Michigan.

Glancing left and right, I expected to see something—any-thing—glowing outside my window or at a distance . . . but the backyard was as dark as it usually was at that time of night. Well, except for the faint intermittent flicker, on my far left, that I saw every night. It came from the string of lights stretching from our roof down to Rosey Hampton's fence. The half of the bulbs clos-est to my bedroom were completely out. My mother bragged that we didn't have a 'who's-got-the-best-Christ-mas-decor-skills-on-my-block' kind of neighborhood. But we sort of did, judging by the complaints about our lights and the constant offers to help fix them before the subdivision holiday parade. The Thompson house was failing miserably.

I climbed back into my bed, pulled the covers up to my chin, and again tried to go to sleep. My family had to leave for the airport early the next morning because, as we did almost every year, me and my brother, Leif, were leaving North Car-olina to go to Michigan and visit with our grandmother until New Year's Day.

"Why can't we go with you to Jamaica?" I had asked my mother as she twirled away into her closet and came back with a slinky dress on a satin hanger.

"Because you haven't seen your grandmother in a long time. You didn't go last year. She misses you, and it's good for you to spend some quality time with her," she replied, her crimson suitcase zipping closed with a sense of finality.

"Then you should be there too. You're her daughter."

"Come on, Alaina. Don't be like that. Your grandmother loves you and I know you're going to have a ball." She nudged me playfully. "And you know you love her cooking."

It was true. The mere thought of my grandmother's pots and pans clanking in the kitchen made my mouth water and brought back memories of cinnamon, nutmeg, sage, and the other scents her home was filled with over the holidays.

"What do parents do for two weeks in Jamaica without their children? Won't you be bored?" asked Leif.

"They do whatever they want," she replied, "without anyone yelling, 'Mom, Mama, Ma, can I? Will you? She just—! He won't—!' all day long." She changed her pitch, mimicking me and Leif, as she said it. Leif fell over laughing. I wasn't amused.

"Plus, we will be going to several islands, not just Jamaica," she added.

It wasn't fair. Who cared about going to Michigan when my best friend, Penelope, had planned out our whole winter break, assuming I wasn't going out of town this year, and I didn't want to miss it. So I tried my best to think of every excuse I could to stay home. "Mom, in case you haven't noticed. I'm practically grown. We don't need a babysitter."

She stopped gathering jewelry from her drawer and pointed at me. "No. Don't even think about it."

Okay, that didn't work. Time to hit her with the big guns. "I'm only thirteen, and in this day and time, two kids have no business flying off to places by themselves. Anything could happen to us. We could end up in Alaska."

"Or Canada," Leif chimed.

"'In this day in time?'" my mom asked and laughed. "A few minutes ago you said you were 'practically grown.' Anyway, you won't be by yourselves. I'm going too . . ."

I grinned. "You are?" *She changed her mind? Then why go? We could all stay home, and grandma could come to our house instead.*

". . . Then your dad and I catch our connecting flight," she added.

"I thought you meant— Aww man . . ."

"I can't wait to go," said Leif, pouncing onto our parent's bed, as our mother exited the room with her makeup case.

"You're always on her side," I whispered to him.

"Well, she's usually right about things."

"Parents aren't always right."

"Yes, they are," Leif shot back.

"No, they aren't."

"Yes, they are."

We carried on like that until I pushed past him and went down the hall to my bedroom. He followed, and I closed the door in his face.

Leif stood on the other side repeating, "Yes, they are," over and over.

I dove onto my bed on my stomach, squeezing pillows over my ears.

"Please snow enough that flights are canceled," I prayed. "Send a blizzard."

Unfortunately, no one was listening.

"Alaina!" my mother yelled several times within a half hour.

"Coming!" I finally left my room with my bags, which were supposed to have been set at the front door the night before.

On my way downstairs, I stood in the hallway, suitcase in one hand, and lifting my backpack over my shoulder with the other. Soft instrumental music drifted through the house. If my mother was trying to calm my nerves about going to Michigan, it was working. I leaned against the wall and closed my eyes. The music was like a glimpse of heaven, a serene reminder that God was real and present.

"Alaina!" she yelled once more.

My eyes flashed open. "Coming!"

I trudged down the stairs and into the kitchen.

"So we're not doing happy today?" asked my father, brushing his barely-there hair.

"This *is* happy, Dad."

He turned to my mom, hearing the jingle of her car keys.

Oh, no. Here we go. That jingle signaled the start of their usual argument about airport trips. Mom insisted on hiring a rideshare car to save on parking fees. Dad's counter argument was always that hiring a car to take us to and from the airport would cost just as much as parking our car there.

"I'll solve this," I said and tossed a nickel in the air. "Heads or tails?"

"Tails!" Dad yelled.

The nickel seemed to hang for a moment before starting its descent. I caught the coin and slapped it on the back of my hand. "Call it."

"Heads!" Mom said.

I lifted my hand, and Mom leaned over the counter to see. "Tails," she said with a sigh. "Fine, we'll take the car."

He shot her a smug smile as she scooped up her keys. "It just makes more sense. Now let's get a move on before we hit traffic."

We did beat the rush hour traffic. And it wasn't until we were at the airport with our boarding passes and going through security that the trouble started. Dad nudged me. "Watch this."

"Is this your bag, Ma'am?" a TSA agent asked.

"Yes. Yes, it is."

The agent unzipped the side pocket and pulled a steak knife from my mother's carry-on bag.

Her face went pale. "Oh my stars. How did that get in there?" She turned to my father. "Tye? Did you—"

He chuckled. Leave it to my dad to try and sneak something past airport security just for laughs. After lots of eye-rolling and apologies, we were finally cleared to head to our gate.

The two hours before boarding dragged on endlessly. Leif and I plopped down on the hard plastic airport seats while my parents grabbed coffee and snacks. I pulled out my phone and texted back and forth with Penelope:

Me: *I'm not going.*

Penelope: You'd better.

Me: *I'm going to find a way to stay. I'll hide.*

Penelope: *Yeah, that's the mature thing to do.*

Over the intercom, an airline attendant announced that our flight was delayed another thirty minutes due to in-clement weather. I suddenly perked up. Maybe my prayers were finally being answered. *Yay, God!* But eventually, the announcement crackled through the airport loudspeakers that we could start boarding, and before I knew it, we were air-borne and headed to Michigan.

I glanced out the window as the plane climbed into the clouds, a strange feeling settling in my stomach. Something about this trip felt . . . off. And it wasn't just the turbulence.

Chapter Two

The wheels of the SUV crunched over the road salt as we neared Grandma Eleanor's house. She'd picked us up from the airport with lots of hugs and then a "Hurry along," as she rushed ahead of us without even helping us with our bags.

Somehow, Michigan was colder than I remembered. I shivered and hugged myself. The fact that we had snow this year in North Carolina should have told me Michigan practically had daily blizzards. Lake-effect snow was what they called it on the radio weather update. We weren't prepared for the difference in weather, but my grandmother was. "Look in the back seat," she said.

On the floor beside Leif was a Target bag stuffed with winter gear. Leif reached inside and grabbed a white hat.

I snatched it from him. "That's for girls. You take the blue one."

"The color doesn't matter. I can have whichever I want, right Grandma?"

"That's right, Leify-Poo."

Liefy Poo? That's why he's so spoiled!

Grandma Eleanor glanced at me, noticing my pout. "But how about we let Alaina have that one, just to be nice."

"Oh, all right," Leif replied with a huff.

I stared out the window as the car parked. The neighborhood was like a snow globe that had just settled, all sparkly and quiet. Although I didn't show it, I was excited to get inside and see if Grandma Eleanor had cooked anything. I had refused the snacks on the plane–pretzels, and there were no other options. I was on a quest not to eat anything pre-packaged. Only homemade foods were going in my body.

"Look, Alaina! It's even bigger than last time!" Leif pressed his nose against the frosty window, leaving a smudge that looked a bit like a lopsided fingerprint.

"Grandma says houses grow just like people do," I replied, though I knew it wasn't entirely true. As I got older, I thought most houses seemed smaller. Her house *was* wider now though. I had overheard my mom saying she added an addition to the house.

Leif stared up at the upstairs windows, and I was pretty sure it was because he wanted to get to Grandma's attic as soon as possible in search of undiscovered treasures. It was a game he played every time we visited.

We jumped out of the car, our shoes landing in the snow with twin thuds. The cold air nipped at my nose and cheeks.

Leif ran around the car and his mittened hand found mine, pulling me forward.

"Race you to the door!" he challenged, released my hand, and shot off.

"Hey, no fair!" I wasn't really going to run anywhere. Slip and fall on the ice? No thank you.

"Don't you have bags in the back?" asked our grandmother.

"Oh, our suitcases and backpacks. Leif, come back!"

He responded by running back and tossing a handful of loose snow in my direction, which I dodged with a squeal. At seven years old and full of mischief, I should have expected it.

Grandma Eleanor shut her car door. "Save the snowball fights for later. Get your bags and go inside. Let's get you unpacked and settled in."

Once we closed the hatch and grabbed our things, Leif was ready to race again, though he could barely run with the weight of the bags. We reached the porch at the same time, a jumble of giggles and snowy footprints.

Grandma Eleanor stood in the doorway removing her coat and scarf. The silver in her hair shone like fairy strands against her dark hair.

"Welcome back to Shiloh, my dears!" She pulled us into an embrace that smelled of flowers, and I felt something inside me unwind—a knot I hadn't realized was there until it was gone.

Shiloh. I forgot my grandmother had a name for her house. The whole fifteen acres actually.

"Grandma!" Leif said, his voice muffled against her sweater. "I've missed you!"

"And I you, my little Leif" she replied, ruffling his hair which sprang back into place as if it too were excited to be there.

I unzipped my coat. "You guys just went through that whole greeting at the airport."

"So what?" said Leif.

"That was a welcome to Michigan. This is a welcome back to my home—your home for the next few weeks. I'm sure I will think of more reasons to steal a hug as the day goes on."

Grandmother Eleanor's fingers, slender and sure, beckoned us forward. The foyer loomed with its high ceilings and chandelier. The floor was a chessboard of black and white tiles.

"And that wasn't funny," she said, "you asking me for ID at the airport to prove who I was or you were going to call security."

I giggled. "We joke. That's what we do in this family."

Grandma Eleanor raised an eyebrow, but a smile tugged at her lips. "Well, next time, joke with your parents. You're lucky I didn't leave you right there at the airport."

"Now, that would have been funny," said Leif.

"Shoes off," Grandma Eleanor said, looking at our feet. "And those sneakers will never do here. We're going to have to get you some decent boots."

Leif hopped on one foot, struggling to tug off a shoe. I helped steady him before removing my own and placed them neatly against the baseboard.

"Mind the elephant!" Grandma Eleanor chuckled, pointing to an ornate umbrella stand that glowered at us with stony eyes. I eyed the creature warily—its gaze seemed too knowing, too watchful. Creepy.

A warm draft wrapped around us, guiding us away from the foyer and into the next room. Through the next entrance, the living room unfolded before us. Heavy drapes framed the windows, and there were plush armchairs in different areas that I imagined were for private conversations during dinner parties, because this was a dinner party room if I'd ever seen one.

"Ooh, look!" Leif scampered toward the fireplace where flames crackled and popped. He held his hands out and warmed them. Then he moved on, bounding over to inspect the twinkling Christmas tree tucked in the corner and reaching higher than any tree I had ever seen in someone's home. This was the type of tree you would see in the center of the rotunda at our shopping mall. It was beautiful and covered in ornate golden butterflies.

"Grandma, you left this fire going while you came to pick us up from the airport?" I asked.

Suddenly, a woman walked into the room and introduced herself as Mintz. Her pumps clicked across the floor as she neared us. She wore neat pants and a button-down shirt that looked freshly ironed. Her dark hair had lighter streaks in it that framed her face, and not one hair of her bob was out of place. In other words, she looked super put-together. She had a pleasant smile that contrasted with her serious demeanor and referred to herself as Grandma Eleanor's assistant. "No, that was me. I wanted to make sure the room was nice and toasty when you arrived." With a wink, Mintz hurried off down the hall and disappeared through a doorway.

I turned my attention back to the fire. My fingers trailed over the mantel piece; a stage set for photos in antique-looking frames. Most of them were from our winter breaks spent with Grandma Eleanor and our school photos.

Although I had fussed and pouted about the trip for the past month, pretty much had a tantrum the night before, and whined the whole flight over, I was happy to be at Shiloh and smiled at the photos of us, much younger, and covered in flour and cookie dough.

Our grandmother exited the room. "Let's continue the tour."

Grandma Eleanor was a grandmother, but didn't look like one, except for her graying hair. I mean, she didn't look anything like our dad's mom. Grandma Ruth was short and round with no wrinkles but a mop of gray locks, and she always smelled of lotion or ointment. But Grandma Eleanor—she was different, youthful. Many people found her odd or unusual. Actually, that's what I loved about her.

I looked up at the wooden slats of the coffered ceiling. The house was different now. Rooms had been redecorated or enlarged, and ceilings raised since our last visit. But there was another thing I noticed as we went from room to room. "Uh, Grandma, we have a problem."

"What is it, Alaina?"

"I haven't seen a television. Do you even have cable?"

"No."

"What? What are we supposed to do here?" In that whole huge house, we found one television, and it was tiny. For all I knew it was an old computer monitor.

"Live, is what you'll do," she replied with a smirk.

"What?" I thought I was going to have a heart attack. I needed to. At least then I would end up in the hospital where there is television. In my head, I went over every scenario I could think of to not have to endure this house for two weeks. *Mom, the house is haunted. I have the flu. There are rats everywhere. Can you come and get me? Leif is sick. Leif fell out of a window. He has internal bleeding.*

"Follow me," Grandma said, running and sliding through an arched doorway. *Did she really just do that?* For a second,

I thought we were having a Willie Wonka moment and were going to follow her into a Chocolate room where everything was edible. Leif grabbed one of the warm chocolate chip cookies from a plate on a table and held it toward me to see if I wanted a bite. I rolled my eyes. I didn't want a cookie; I wanted dinner and then Netflix.

Leif took a bite. Crumbs tumbled down the front of his sweater as he turned and followed Grandma, running and sliding.

With a sigh, I followed too. *Why me?* I screamed inside. Why couldn't my family be normal? We always did things differently than everyone else. Breakfast might be spaghetti, and dinner might be something weird like chitterlings.

We entered a long hallway lined with paintings and sculptures. I peered at a portrait of a man with long white hair, whose eyes seemed to follow me as I passed. I'd seen them all on previous visits, but this time he stood out. Maybe I hadn't paid much attention before.

At the end of the hall was an ornate set of double doors. *We're going in there?* Grandma took an antique key from her pocket and unlocked the doors with a heavy click.

Yep, the Chocolate room.

As the doors swung open, my mouth dropped at the sight of the enormous room with floor-to-ceiling bookshelves. Every shelf and wall was painted emerald green. I slowly spun around. "You've never let us in here before."

"That's because you were too young to appreciate it. These books are the most precious things I own."

I walked around the room reading the spines of books I had never heard of: *Secrets in View*, *The Undimmed Light*, and *The Gift of the King* by author Stephen Woodruff. In all my thirteen years, I had never even attempted to enter the room. Grandma Eleanor kept it locked and told us it was empty.

Suddenly, my mind shifted from intrigue to shock. "Is this what we're supposed to do for two whole weeks?" I turned to Leif, expecting him to co-sign on my complaint, representing a united front. But he was already gone. He didn't care about books. He would go somewhere in the house and build a fort out of anything he could find.

Grandma Eleanor walked toward me. I looked down at the soft area rug, my cheeks burning with regret, expecting to be scolded for what I had said. Instead, she gently lifted my chin and stared into my eyes for so long that it became awkward.

"Grandma—"

"Shh . . . Do. Not. Move." That oddness she was known for was kicking in. Then, suddenly, she dropped her finger. "I think you're going to be just fine," she said and walked out of the room.

Chapter Three

I hesitated, giving the room one last glance before following my grandmother out. The heavy doors closed with a soft thud behind me, but something made me pause. I noticed they didn't lock without the key.

I caught up to Grandma Eleanor in the kitchen, where she started telling funny stories about her youth, growing up in Muskegon, and Leif couldn't stop giggling. But then, like always, she ended up telling some weird story that creeped me out. "Have you ever thought you saw something, but when you looked, nothing was there?" she asked.

"Yes," I replied. "Usually, it's just a strand of my hair that I see from the corner of my eye, or nothing at all."

"That's what I used to think. But now, I know differently."

"What is it," asked Leif while trying to scoop up chili with a cheese covered fry.

"No, I don't think I'm going to tell you. You won't believe me. Let's talk about something else."

Leif hopped out of his chair. "No, tell us!"

"No, I think you're too young to hear about this. I shouldn't have brought it up."

I plopped against the backrest of my chair. *Please stop with the reverse psychology already. You know you're going to tell us.*

"All right, I'll tell you." Grandma Eleanor leaned toward Leif and whispered loud enough for both of us to hear. "It's really angels—looking out for us."

I crunched on the ice I had poured into my mouth from my glass. "Angels?"

"Yep."

Leif looked at me for confirmation with his eyes wide. I shook my head at him. Grandma Eleanor was always making things up.

Then she said, "Remember the time you were talking to angels?"

I almost choked on my ice. "What do you mean? I don't remember that."

"You're weird," said Leif.

"You were about four or five. I remember finding you in the garden, standing by the flowers, having a full-on conversation. I thought you were just pretending, but when I asked who you were talking to, you looked at me and said, 'The angels, Grandma. They're so pretty.'"

"I must have been sleepwalking or something," I suggested.

"No, my dear, you were wide awake."

"So what happened?"

"I knelt beside you," Grandma Eleanor replied mysteriously. She stopped there, like that was the end of the story, while my eyes were wide waiting for what she was going to say next.

"And what happened?" asked Leif.

Grandma Eleanor picked up her plate and walked over to the sink, and I thought I was going to pull my hair out waiting for her to reply.

"You had a huge smile. The whole thing was pretty special. You said they were singing to you and telling you that you were loved. I'll never forget how innocent and happy you were. It was like you were having your own little bit of heaven right there."

I almost fell out of my chair. "You are hilarious, Grandma."

"Forgive me if I'm not laughing with you, but that's exactly what you told me, and I believed you."

I shrugged. *I said that? What did I know? I was five years old and still talking to dolls and horrified by Teletubbies.*

Grandma Eleanor didn't say any more about the memory as if she wanted it to brew for a while. I didn't know what good that would do. I didn't remember the incident at all. Nor did I want to. I wanted a television.

I helped clean up the kitchen that evening, which surprised my grandmother. I would have done it on my own, but my mom had already lectured me that I'd better act like she'd taught us to have good manners and help out.

As soon as I finished, the phone rang, and I grabbed it from the counter before Leif could. "Hello?"

"Alaina?"

"Hey, Mom!" She always knew when to call. I wouldn't be surprised if she had a camera somewhere watching us.

"You sound happy. Are you having a good time? Are you watching your manners?"

"Yes, I am—"

"Let me talk to her," said Leif, pulling at the phone.

"Hold on a minute," I told him and moved the phone to my other ear. "We had an early dinner, and I mean good stuff," I told my mom. "One of the two kitchen islands—"

"There are two islands now?"

"Yep, and one of them was covered in food. All of our favorites from Grandma Eleanor's recipes: lasagna, peach cobbler, chili cheese fries, beanie weenies, a charcuterie board . . ."

"Charcuterie board? Please tell me your grandmother didn't have wine."

"Like I would tell on her, if she did. But no."

My mother laughed. "Okay, well you didn't mention one vegetable."

"There were lots of veggies, but I was the only one interested in them."

"Give it here," said Leif. "I have stuff to tell too."

"Mom, Leif wants to talk to you." I handed him the phone, and he snatched it as if I wasn't handing it over.

It was late when we finally got ready for bed. We took baths in the ensuite of our bedrooms. I filled my tub with warm water and bubbles while Leif preferred plain water in his saying, "Shark divers can't see through bubbles."

After he promised me he would actually scrub his body *and* use soap, I left him to splash away. He would stay in there for a good hour acting like Aquaman until Grandma Eleanor or I made him get out.

After my bath, I dressed in my flannel pajamas and robe, grabbed my Tangle Brush and detangled my hair (my least favorite thing to do because it hurt), and then twisted my hair into two neat braids. Next, I checked to see if my phone was charged so I could at least watch YouTube videos. It wasn't. It only had 15% battery left and the screen showed a notification that it was in low power mode. I unplugged the charger from the wall and inserted it again into the socket. Nothing happened. Just my luck, a bad socket in a practically totally remodeled house.

I went to check on Leif and found him sprawled at the foot of his bed, snoring. I covered him with a blanket and went back to my room. Along the way, I paused for a moment outside Grandma Eleanor's room but there was no sound coming from inside, so I continued down the hall.

These bedrooms had always been ours and kept exactly the same until our return. My room was filled with drawings from over the years and toys from all the times we had visited. Leif's room was filled with dinosaurs and STEM building toys, a replica of what he had at our house. Grandma Eleanor's really was a home away from home.

I knew I was tired. I had barely slept the night before, and now it weighed on my eyelids. But no matter how much I tried, I couldn't get to sleep. Instead, I lay there staring at the ceiling. Despite spending countless summers, winters, and spring breaks there as a child, the place still felt foreign for the first few days.

Eventually, somehow, I drifted off and awoke to the house being totally dark and completely silent. Either we lost power, or my grandmother still did her rounds at night turning off every light in the house.

I sat up and swept my phone's flashlight around my room. The beam shone over the cluttered desk, my still packed suitcase, and the half-open closet door, revealing nothing out of place and no intruder lurking while I slept. Then I heard a faint, muffled sound just outside my door, like a soft shuffle. I crept toward it and pressed my ear against the wood, straining to catch any hint of movement. But there were no other sounds. I cautiously turned the knob, the door creaking softly on its hinges as it opened, and I went out into the hall. I had expected to find Leif standing there, but the hall was empty. His door was closed, and no light shone from underneath it.

A clinking sound came from the stairs, and I carefully walked that way, hoping my phone battery wouldn't die and leave me in the dark. I followed the curve of the stairs, my hand clutching the black glossy rail, until I got to the bottom landing. Then I walked away from the front door towards the back of the house, shining my light into each room as I passed. Some monster wasn't going to get me without me seeing it coming. For that reason, I shone the light behind me every few steps.

At the entrance to the back hall I stopped walking, looking straight ahead at the light that crept out from under the huge doors to the library. It pulsed like a heartbeat. I hesitated, wondering if I should run and get my grandmother, but then I realized it was probably her in there, reading. *But what would make her lamp pulse like that?*

I tiptoed to the doors, and slowly pulled on the handle. It was still unlocked. I expected to open the door and see Grandma Eleanor sitting in one of the big recliners, looking at me with an expression that asked, "What are you doing up, skulking around the house in the middle of the night?"

The light shut off as the door opened. I lifted my phone around the room trying to find a light switch, but it wasn't necessary. On the table in the center of the room was a book . . . and it started glowing.

This wasn't there earlier today, I thought, walking up to the table.

Every time I looked away. The room became dark. When I looked at the book again, it glowed. *Am I causing this?*

My fingers traced the textured black leather cover, stopping at the delicate golden butterfly emblem in the center. I gently grasped the edge of the cover, as if it would fall apart if I handled it too roughly, and opened it. The faint light that was left totally disappeared.

Pfft. I chuckled. *Grandma Eleanor is such a trickster. She got me this time.* I set my phone on the table so that the light was shining up at the ceiling and lifted the book searching for wires that connected to the table or a battery source. There were none.

I set the book down, half-expecting that at any moment it would whisk me away into some fantastical adventure. It looked like a normal book but older. I picked up my phone and sat with the book on my lap, noticing the 7% battery warning flashing on the screen. As I read, my surroundings faded away, replaced by the vivid imagery painted by the words on the page.

It was as if a portal had opened before my eyes, revealing a world where reality intertwined with fantasy, drawing me in like a whisper in the night.

The story told of a girl in Muskegon by the name of Sheena Meyer, the same age as me. *And she attends Nelson school?* I had heard of it. The school went from kindergarten to eighth grade. Several of the friends I made at the youth center when we came to visit before, attended Nelson.

I continued reading about her life and friends and how she had a special gift. The story was getting interesting.

Wait, what? I grinned, again thinking someone was playing a trick on me. *This isn't possible.* I read on. Suddenly, I hopped out of my seat, dropping the book from my lap. *That's not possible. How is this in this book?*

The book told of a girl and her brother arriving at their grandmother's house while their parents were having a second honeymoon vacation in the Caribbean.

The girl's name was . . . Alaina. I backed away, staring at the open book on the floor watching the pages turn as if wind blew them. *My name? Is it me? How could it be talking about me?*

I shot out of there, down the hall, through the next, up the stairs and dove into my bed, pulling my covers up under my chin, clasping them tightly there. *That didn't just happen. I'm asleep. I'm dreaming, I thought as I squeezed my eyes shut.*

Suddenly, my eyes shot open. *Oh no! What did I do? I left my grandmother's book on the floor? One of her prized possessions?* I knew what her books meant to her. What had I done? The last thing I wanted was to be grounded for the whole trip. I needed to go back down there and get it off the floor, but it wasn't going to happen while it was still night.

Eventually, I fell asleep with all of the lights on in my room. When I awoke, because of the updates to the house, I half expected to open my eyes to the sound of live violinists and to find a lady's maid waiting at the foot of the bed with my freshly ironed clothes.

I yawned, suddenly remembering what had happened just a few hours before. I saw the time and clasped my hand over my mouth. Grandma Eleanor had probably already gone into the library.

This situation required a pep talk—totally out of character for me: *It wasn't your fault. The book scared you. It was glowing and the story was about you. Anyone would have freaked out. Go and tell Grandma Eleanor exactly what happened. She will understand. Yeah, I think I will.*

After a couple of panicked gulps of air, I slipped my feet into my slippers, on loan to me from Grandma Eleanor, and left the room. I stood at the top of the stairs, my hands gripping the banister tightly. *Oh, just do it already*, I told myself and hurried down to the library. The door was closed. I turned the handle and opened the door as quietly as I could, stepped inside, and walked over to the center of the room. The book was back on the pedestal.

She found it already? All that I could do now was own up to it. So I went straight to the kitchen and waited for my grandmother to reprimand us and ask who had done it—probably assuming it was Leif.

Instead, true to our family weirdness, she was spooning out Jello and mini marshmallows for breakfast.

"It's what Leif asked for," Grandma Eleanor told me, responding to the question on my face. Jazz Christmas music played on the radio, and the tea kettle went off on one of the eight burners of the gas stove. I inched my way over to one of the two islands and sat, waiting for my scolding.

Grandma Eleanor walked over and popped me on the forehead.

"Oww," I said and grabbed my head, though it didn't hurt at all.

"Snap out of it," she said. "Did you sleep okay?"

"Yes. I-I . . ." I couldn't bring myself to say it. I think I was too stunned by the head pop. There was one thing about me that my family knew. I didn't like getting in trouble. As a result, I avoided anything that would put me in a place of being yelled at, grounded, or when I was little, getting a spanking. I didn't like the looks of disappointment from the people who believed in me. It made me feel like I had let them down, so I would burst into tears and wallow in depression for days. My antics were worse than any punishment. So telling my grandmother about the book, considering she didn't seem to know anything about what happened...was out of the question. "I slept okay."

"Good. What will it be for breakfast?"

"You mean I don't have to eat Jello and marshmallows?"

"Not if you don't want to."

"Wow. My mom would say, 'This is what we have, so this is what you are eating.'"

"Do I look like your mom?"

"Yes," said Leif. "Your eyes and your smile."

"That's true, I replied."

"No. What I'm saying is, I do things my way in my home. So what will it be, Alaina?"

"A slice of your sweet potato pie and whipped cream?"

"I like how you think. Coming right up."

That was too easy. She knows I did it and is trying to torture me. What am I going to do?

The whole day passed, and Grandma Eleanor never said anything about the book, so I didn't either. *Why interrupt all the fun with bad news and spoil the mood?* Maybe Mintz found it and picked it up. Perhaps that was part of her job as an assistant. But if no one was going to mention it, I sure wouldn't. And though I vowed to never go back into the library again, I found myself back in there that night with a flashlight, reading over the titles of other books, avoiding the one I knew I came in there for. Finally, I walked over to the center of the room, carefully lifted the book from the table, and sat in a large brown velvet club chair.

My finger glided over the grainy pages and stopped. *She's in danger?* The story told that something was after Sheena Meyer. "What is it?" I asked aloud.

I noticed a zip of light from the corner of my eye and looked in that direction. In a split second, everything around me blurred together and the library disappeared.

What is happening? "Grandma Eleanor," I tried to scream, but the words got caught in my throat. The house was so huge; who knew if she would even hear me if I screamed?

Suddenly, I was in a field at night, looking up at the stars. I glanced all around me. The wind blew, but it wasn't cold, and I could feel the earth beneath my feet like I was really there. Out of nowhere, a massive shadow loomed over me, growing and expanding into the sky, churning and blotting out the stars. It was like a living, smokey furnace. *Run!* I told myself. But before I could react, it hurled towards me with an ear-splitting screech. I screamed and felt my body go limp as I slipped into unconsciousness.

My eyes snapped open, and I gasped for air, awaking in my bed with my comforter twisted around me like a straitjacket. The sun was already up and shining through the windows. *How did I get here?*

The book ... That thing ... Was it real? Did the book have some kind of power to transport me into its stories? *No. That's not what happened. It couldn't.* I thought for a moment. "I asked what Sheena Meyer was in danger from and it showed me."

Chapter Four

My heart pounded in my chest as I fought off the suffocating grip of my comforter and kicked it to the end of the bed. Sweat rolled down my neck and beneath my pajama shirt as I sat up. As soon as my feet hit the floor, a surge of panic filled me and I ran back and forth across the room. "Did I dream it all? I couldn't possibly make that up. Could I?" I had never been much of a storyteller. Although, I did have an overactive imagination.

I rifled through my backpack, hoping I had packed my power bank, and let a sigh of relief when I found it. "Yes!" I exclaimed, grabbing my phone and plugging it in. Within 60 seconds, it had just enough charge for me to use it. "Call Penelope."

The phone barely rang before she picked up. "Alaina? What's up, deserter? Are you having fun?" She asked without saying hello and yawned. "You'd better be. It's so early. I haven't been up long. We're going ice skating today. You're going to miss it. Noah will probably be there, and you know Christine likes him too. At least I think she does. I'll tell him you said hello. How's Muskegon—I mean, Michigan? Wait, Muskegon is in Michigan, right? It's too early for geography. Have you finished your Christmas shopping? Is Leif being a pain?"

"Penelope! Have you had an energy drink or something? Stop talking. I need to tell you something." I pictured her dramatically flinging the end of her Santa nightcap out of her face and sitting up straight. She wore those hats around the clock until Christmas every year. She was all-things-holidays, like her mom, which wasn't a bad thing, but right now, I needed her holly jolly-self to calm down. Her jabbering was only going to make me more homesick. And don't get me started on Noah. It wasn't like he even knew I existed or that I had a major crush on him (like I would ever tell him). Instead of being there to watch him effortlessly skate by in his hoodie and red scarf with his hair all perfectly twisted, I was clear in another state, at my grandmother's house, dealing with some crazy mystical book. *Ugh, why is my life such a fantasy movie cliché?*

The whole thing was so real—the musty old book lighting up and then me appearing somewhere else and the dark plume rising into the wintery night sky. But now, in the light of day, it seemed impossible. Yet I awoke in my bed. *How did I get here?* I shook my head, trying to clear the cobwebs.

"Alaina?"

"Huh?"

"You were going to tell me something" Penelope replied.

"Oh..." I took a deep breath to gather my thoughts. "Pen, something really weird happened last night."

"What happened?"

"I was reading this old book I found in my grandmother's library and it like . . . transported me into the story. And then this huge, smoky creature rose up and started coming after me! It was terrifying. I passed out and then woke up here in my bed?"

"At your house?"

"No, at my grandmother's house. Do you think it was just a crazy dream, or could it have actually happened?"

Penelope was silent for a moment.

"Pen? Penelope?"

She burst out laughing. I stood there and listened to her howl for a good two minutes. Just when I was about to hang up, she said, "I'm sorry," catching her breath. "That's your best one yet."

It was an accurate response. I mean, I came from a family of practical jokers. Trickery was inbred.

My voice was serious. "Pen, I'm not joking."

Penelope was silent for a moment. "Woah," she finally said. "You're not lying?"

"If I'm lying, I'm frying," I told her (something my dad says).

"That sounds freaky. But also kind of awesome? Do you think the book is magic or something?"

"I don't know what it is, but I am never touching that thing again."

"You have to." Penelope's voice lit up. "If this is like a real fantasy story, you have to figure out what it's showing you and why. You have to keep reading. You know what? We may not be able to use AI chatbots for school assignments, but you can use it for this. Ask one what to do. My mom is calling me. Be careful, okay? Don't let any giant smoke monsters get you."

"Pen, you can't tell anyone about this."

"Who am I gonna tell? Keep me posted on what happens."

I smiled slightly. "Thanks, Pen. Talk to you later? Penelope?" My phone died.

I'd had most of the same friends since second grade, when we moved from Michigan because of my father's job. But Penelope was my favorite of them all. We understood each other. We agreed that boys were scum—until, like, last year. And she had her priorities in order: nothing was more important than whatever I was into at the moment—not saying Penelope was a follower. She was just down for whatever.

I glanced uneasily at my door. "See what it wants me to know?"

When I was younger, I thought there was something special about being at Shiloh. Back then, it was impossible to truly worry for long periods within these walls. A safe haven was the only way to describe my grandmother's home until this moment. Now I sat with bubble guts as my thoughts were interrupted by the sound of pounding feet racing up the hall. My bedroom door burst open, and Leif came barreling in, sliding in his footed pajamas.

"Wake up, sleepyhead!" he shouted, jumping onto my bed.

"I was already up. Why are you bothering me?"

"Because breakfast is ready and Grandma Eleanor told me to come and get you."

"Leif, why are you wearing those? Those are your Christmas pajamas. You're not supposed to wear those until Christmas Eve."

He pulled at the stomach of his pine tree-covered pjs. "They're warm. And this is from last year. It's not the new ones."

"Oh, that would explain why it fits you like a spiderman suit."

"It does? Cool! Let's go eat."

"First, you need to get dressed."

"Are *you* getting dressed?"

"Of course," I replied, pulling a sweatshirt and pants out of my suitcase. Leif ran out of my room. "Put on your thermals too!" I yelled.

He changed fast and was already downstairs when I walked into the kitchen.

"Good morning," Nana said and bumped me with her hip as I glided by. Her hands were behind her back. She wore a sweatshirt too, with a turtleneck beneath it showing from the collar. "You look like you've got a lot on your mind this morning, Alaina. Or is that hunger I see?"

"Not really . . . I-I—"

"Maybe you would enjoy exploring the grounds this morning with Leif."

"Are you trying to traumatize me?"

"How do you mean? Have you never gone for a walk or played in the snow?"

"Not since I was a kid. I'm almost an adult."

Grandma Eleanor snickered. "Adult, huh?"

"You can't send me out to play like I'm a child, Grandma. I babysit children. I'm not a child."

"Someone allowed *you* to babysit? Give me their names and numbers so I can call them and ask if they've lost their mind."

My mouth hung open. She really didn't believe I was mature enough to babysit?

"Who have you babysat?"

"Uh . . . Leif."

"That's what I thought," she replied.

Sheesh, I could babysit. It's just that no one ever asked me.

"Oww!" I exclaimed.

I didn't see where it came from, but a wad of snow hit me on the side of my head. My eyes widened in shock. "Did you just—?"

Leif pointed and laughed.

"What are you going to do about it," Grandma Eleanor asked as she backed out of the kitchen and through the mudroom.

I moved away from the counter to where I could see out of the door. As soon as I did, another snowball hit me in the stomach.

Like I said, she wasn't like other grandmothers, and she could still run. That's when I noticed she was already wearing boots.

I charged out of the kitchen, behind Leif, stopping only to pull on my sneakers and grab any coat within reach. And though I was thirteen and too old for these shenanigans, we had the best snowball fight ever.

We were all cold ears, pink runny noses, and numb lips when we finally made it back inside. On the way in, Grandma Eleanor collected a bucket of fresh snow that we eyed curiously.

Mugs of hot chocolate were waiting for us on the kitchen counter. I had forgotten about Mintz until I saw her leave through the entrance to the living room and wondered when she came and left, or whether she was always there.

Grandma Eleanor set the bucket of snow beside the sink, along with a gallon of milk, a bag of sugar, sea salt, and a bottle of vanilla extract.

"What are you doing?" I asked, rubbing my defrosting hands together.

"What does it look like? I'm making ice cream."

"Out of snow? Is that safe to eat?"

"Of course it is. It's a clean bucket."

"No, I'm talking about what falls from the sky. Isn't it falling through pollution?"

"Trust me, you'll be fine. What you have to do is set a clean bucket outside as soon as it starts snowing, like I did. Go and put on some dry clothes. We're having fresh ice cream for lunch. I've got a ton of toppings."

"Yay!" Leif exclaimed.

"By the time we get home, we're going to need to go to the dentist," I mumbled as Leif and I climbed the stairs.

All day, I never mentioned what happened to me in the library or what I saw. But just like the night before, I stirred from my sleep in the wee hours of the morning and glanced at my clock. 3 a.m. I slowly climbed out of bed and paused to listen for any noises coming from the rest of the house. Mintz might pop out of nowhere as she often did. But the only sound was the humming of the furnace. I cracked my bedroom door open just enough to squeeze through, as if it wouldn't open any wider. *What are you doing?* I asked myself, shaking my head. I tiptoed down the stairs, wincing at every step. At the bottom I paused, straining to hear any sign that someone else was awake.

Once I was sure I was the only person up and roaming around, I made my way to the library. The polished wooden floor was cold under my bare feet. At the door, I hesitated, fingers resting on the brass door handle. What if that thing returned tonight? No, it wouldn't. *I won't ask about it, so the book won't show me that.*

Curiosity overpowered my fear, and I turned the handle of the library door. Again, I found it unlocked. The room smelled of aged paper, leather bindings, and a hint of pine. The shelves of books towered into the darkness. The only light came from the moonlight through the skylights. I scanned the room warily. Spotting the podium where the mysterious book had rested, I crept closer. It wasn't lighting up this time. When I got to the table, the surface was bare. The book was gone. I released a breath I hadn't realized I was holding as relief and disappointment intertwined within me. *What happened to it?*

That book was the only reason for me to be in the library in the middle of the night, so I turned to leave. A glint caught my eye. There, on the floor by the podium, was a single iridescent feather. *Where did this come from? Someone's coat? A pillow maybe?* My eyes widened as I picked it up and twirled it between my fingers. The feather glowed softly, and I tucked it into my T-shirt pocket.

"Looking for something?"

I jumped and let out a yelp as I spun around to face Grandma Eleanor standing in the doorway with her hand on the knob.

"Grandma! You scared me," I said, trying to catch my breath.

She chuckled. "Why was your first reaction to scream? That's not normal for someone wandering around in the dark. There's nothing to fear at Shiloh. What brings you to the library in the middle of the night?"

I hesitated. "I couldn't sleep."

"Well, I'd say this is the best place to come when that happens. Why don't we sit down for a bit?" She gestured towards the sitting area in one corner of the room.

I followed her and sat on one of the plush chairs. She turned on a small stained-glass lamp on the table between us. "Alaina?"

I stopped biting my lip. "Yes?"

"You look like you have a question. This would be a great time to ask it—when Leif isn't interrupting and you have my undivided attention."

Let's see . . . How can I say this and not sound nuts? "Well . . . Sometimes in life—"

"In life?" she asked and smirked. "You always say things as if you've been on this earth a lot longer than thirteen years."

"That's because I'm almost an adult."

"So you've told me. Go on."

"Sometimes in life things happen that can't be explained."

"I agree."

"You–you do?"

She nodded while looking up at the skylight.

"Then that means . . . I mean . . . Do you believe in magic?"

"No, I don't. But the world is full of things that are pretty baffling."

I straightened in my seat. "Magical things?"

"There is no magic, Alaina," she replied. "There is only the gleam."

Chapter Five

My brows knit in confusion. "The what?"

Grandma Eleanor's pupils glinted, a deep sparkle that I thought I was imagining.

"The gleam," she repeated. Her manicured almond-shaped white nails traced invisible patterns in the air for a moment.

There she goes acting weird.

"A gifting from heaven," she said and reclined her chair.

"I don't know what that means. Are you saying that it looks like magic, but it's this gleam you're talking about?"

"There is no such thing as magic. There is only the gleam."

Suddenly, the room felt smaller. There was something about the way she spoke. This wasn't a joke. I got the feeling she was revealing part of a secret she wasn't ready to share.

I looked away, thinking. When I looked back, Grandma Eleanor's eyes were closed and she lightly snored. Then, from the corner of my eye, I noticed a warm glow. *What? How? She said there's no magic, but a book just appeared out of nowhere and it's lighting up like it has a battery.*

My head snapped toward Grandma Eleanor and back to the book. I stood and glanced at my grandmother again. She didn't stir. I walked over and stared at the book a moment before I carefully picked it up, feeling the smooth leather and then the metallic butterfly emblem against my hand. For some reason, my feet wouldn't let me move from where I was. I sat cross-legged on the floor with a soft glow radiating up at me. The book's pages filled with words. Every sentence mirrored moments from my life—intimate details I had never shared, thoughts and feelings only I knew: The time I sat alone in the cafeteria, pretending to read so no one would see the tears in my eyes. How I told myself it didn't matter that everyone watched me be humiliated when my teacher called on me and I couldn't figure out the math problem. The stuffed animal that was my best friend for far too many years. My mother's mackerel and rice dish that made me want to puke. It even mentioned my crush on Noah.

A shiver ran down my spine. *How is this possible?* A mix of fear and fascination swirled inside me. It was like someone had been spying on me and placed my information in a story. I remembered Penelope's suggestion, took a deep breath, and finally whispered, "What do you want from me?"

For a moment, nothing happened. Then, slowly, the letters on the page rearranged themselves, forming new sentences. My eyes widened as I read:

It is said that it is the hope of our youth that defeats darkness. There is nothing stronger.

I stared at the words. *The hope of our youth?* Though I didn't quite understand, the word dug into my mind, planting a seed. *Okay,* I thought and glanced at Grandma Eleanor, who didn't stir. *That's a start.*

I pulled out my phone, glad I could now charge it using a kitchen outlet, and glanced at the questions I had screenshot from the chatbot. It had given me ten options to ask. I read the first one. "What are you?"

The words formed in front of me, changing the text from what had been on that page: *Alaina sat on the floor of her grandmother's library and read from the Aetates Papilio, although some called it the Gleaming Book.*

"My questions are being answered by placing them within the story. Okay next question. Why me? Why have I discovered the Gleaming Book?"

Though Alaina didn't believe in the Aetates Papilio or anything she read, she asked it a series of questions. She would soon find that those who carry the light of hope can see the path.

"Hold on . . . I carry this light?"

Grandma Eleanor's head turned to the side, and she rested her arms in her lap. I waited to make sure she was still asleep and glanced at the questions on my phone again. "Who is Sheena Meyer, and why does she need help?"

Alaina soon finds that Sheena Meyer's fate and hers are intertwined.

That's very vague. "What happens if I don't help her?"

If Alaina chooses not to accept the mission . . .

Sheena's light will fade, and darkness will strengthen until it consumes everything. The world around her will change, shadows creeping into places that once held brilliant light. But the greatest loss will not be Sheena's; it will be Alaina's.

"Mine? I'm only thirteen. How could this involve me?" My voice shook as I spoke. "How can I help her?"

To help Sheena Meyer, Alaina must first understand herself. Sheena's heart will echo her own. In trusting her instincts, Alaina will know what to do when the time comes.

I gulped and prepared for the final question I wanted to ask from the list—at least for now. "Tell me, but do not show me, what dangers I should be aware of." I almost patted myself on the back. Wording is everything.

The greatest dangers lie not just in the darkness Alaina will face, but also in the doubt that creeps into her heart. Fear may cloud her vision, and despair may tempt her to abandon her mission. She must beware those who seem to help but seek to mislead, and trust only those whose hearts are true. Shadows will test her, but it is her hope and courage that will light the way.

I couldn't say that I understood all of what I read, but I stood and placed the book back on the stand, still open.

The whole time, I thought about how ridiculous it was that I was asking a book questions. And how this gleam thing was allowing it to answer.

"One more thing," I whispered, looking down at the open book. "How do I find Sheena Meyer?"

Seek the path where courage lies,

A name that echoes strength in ties.

On the street where might and valor meet,

There you'll find the girl you seek.

"What?"

CHAPTER SIX

"Grandma, Grandma," I said, gently tapping her leg.

She rubbed her eyes. "Did I fall asleep on you? What is it, Alaina?"

"Come with me. I need to show you something."

"Show me in the morning," she said and scratched her head through her bonnet.

"This is serious." I grabbed her hand and pulled her to the middle of the room. "This book," I replied and pointed. But it wasn't glowing.

"What about it?" she asked.

"I—uh . . . Glow!" I demanded.

"Excuse me?"

She's never going to believe me. "This book—it . . ."

Grandma Eleanor looked alarmed. "Is something wrong with it? Did Leif come in here with frosting on his fingers or something?" she asked as she bent over it and carefully examined the edges.

"No, I just . . . I saw . . . I don't know. Never mind. I think I need a cup of coffee."

"Well that's not going to happen, but maybe you should go back to bed. You look tired. You need to get some sleep and relax your brain for a while. Trust me, by the time you wake up, whatever you're feeling right now will drift away. And if you have a problem, you'll discover the solution. Give it a try," she said with a wink and walked away.

I couldn't disagree with that.

I followed her up the stairs, back to my room, flopped onto the bed, and stared up at the ceiling, replaying the scene in my mind. Grandma Eleanor didn't see the book glowing. It was just a book to her. But it wasn't to me. It said I had a mission. I closed my eyes, remembering:

Seek the path where courage lies,

A name that echoes strength in ties.

On the street where might and valor meet,

There you'll find the girl you seek.

What in the world does that mean? I tossed and turned until I finally crawled under the covers. My gaze drifted to the window. A gentle snowfall had begun, the flakes dancing against the glass. I watched them absently until my eyelids grew heavy.

But just as I was about to doze off, a flash of light outside the window caught my attention, just like the one I had seen at home. I bolted upright, blinking. "What was that?"

There, hovering outside my window, was a tiny winged figure glowing softly with blue energy. It beckoned to me, not with words, but it did. Then it darted away into the night.

Fairies are real? I scrambled out of bed and pressed my nose to the frosty glass, looking off to the left. The winged light flickered in and out of view. I grabbed my robe and took off from my bedroom and down the stairs. In the mudroom, I shoved my feet into a pair of Grandma Eleanor's boots and grabbed my coat from the hook, moving as quickly and quietly as I could.

Once outside, I caught sight of the winged creature flitting between the trees. Grandma Eleanor said there was no magic, but here I was chasing a fairy into the night. But I didn't close the door behind me in case this turned bad and I had to sprint back inside.

This thing led me across the snow and into the woods beyond the yard. Curiosity took over my fear and pushed me to keep going. I needed to know what I was following and where it was leading me.

As I watched it zigzag through the dark woods, my mind raced with possibilities. Was it a fairy? An Alien? A spirit? *No, don't think spooky stuff, Alaina.* An angel sent to guide me on my mission? For some reason, that thought gave me peace.

Suddenly, the light vanished in front of me and I found myself standing in a clearing surrounded by tall trees and total darkness. *In. The. Dark,* I repeated in my head. Panicked, I spun around in circles, trying to find any sign of where it had gone or even the way back to Grandma Eleanor's house. There were no lights left on, so it was not like I could see it off in the distance, like a lighthouse guiding me to shore.

Instantly, a girl stood at the edge of the clearing, her whole body glowing.

I stumbled backwards, almost tripping over a mound of snow.

"Who are you?" she asked in a soft voice.

"I—I'm Alai—Alai—," I stammered.

She tilted her head curiously. "Alai? That's an unusual name."

"No, I'm Alaina," I explained, trying to process what was happening.

She took steps closer to me, studying me intently. And I took more steps backward, about to run.

"You're not from around here," she said.

"No, I'm not," I replied slowly. "I'm visiting my grand-mother for Christmas."

Her eyes lit up with recognition. "Oh! You must be Eleanor's granddaughter."

I nodded. "Yes." *How did she know Grandma Eleanor?*

The girl smiled warmly at me before becoming serious again. "Why have you come looking for me, Alaina?"

"I-I don't know," I admitted, feeling foolish. I pretty much just followed a firefly that I think morphed into this being, without a second thought.

The girl's expression softened, and I didn't know how she got closer to me, but instantly she did, and then reached out to take my hand. "Peace, be still. It is okay, Alaina. I will not hurt you."

Something about her gentle touch and tone put me at ease.

"Who are you?" I finally managed to ask.

She smiled again before responding, "I am a messenger."

"A messenger?" I repeated, confused.

"Yes. I've been sent to aid and guide you on your journey."

"My journey?" I asked incredulously. This whole scene felt like something out of a book.

She nodded solemnly. "It's time for you to start fulfilling your destiny, Alaina."

I couldn't believe what I was hearing. *Start? Destiny?* "What destiny?" I asked.

"That is for you to discover," she replied. "And I believe you already have. But there is something you need to know. The gleam is powerful, but it is hidden."

"Why?"

"To shield its power until the appointed time. There are those assigned to you to help you on your journey. You are not alone. I will see you again soon."

"Wait, where is the gleam hidden?"

"Find Sheena Meyer."

"But wait. Listen to this: Seek the path where courage lies. A name that echoes strength in ties. On the street where might and valor meet, there you'll find the girl you seek. Do you know what that means?"

"Her location," I heard her whisper as she disappeared.

Chapter Seven

Sunlight dragged me out of a deep sleep. I blinked groggily, rubbing my eyes, but the moment I inhaled, I froze. A foul stench hit my nostrils. Groaning, I turned my head and came face to face with Leif's bottom.

"Seriously?" I said through my hand and sat up.

"Huh?" he replied, then turned over and went back to sleep. Leif had been climbing into my bed ever since he moved from a crib to a toddler bed. Now that he was seven years old, he still did, just not as frequently.

As I watched him, I remembered the girl at the edge of the clearing. *All of that was just a dream? What did she tell me?* I replayed the whole scene in my mind. "Location," she had whispered.

I picked up my journal and pen from beside my bed and wrote out the riddle. Then I circled the keywords in each sentence and read them aloud. "Courage. Strength. The street where might and valor meet."

It was right there in front of my face—might, valor, and courage = strength. I grabbed my phone and typed *Strength*

Street in Muskegon into the search engine. Two seconds later, the results showed on the screen: *Your search for Strength Street in Muskegon did not match any data.* But before I could frown, my eyes drifted below the area on the page offering suggestions for refining my search. Among a few ads and featured snippets, one caught my attention: a real estate listing for a property on Strong Avenue.

Wait a minute . . . Strength Street . . . Strong Avenue . . . "That's it!" I exclaimed, causing Leif to stir. I pulled the street up on my map app noticing it wasn't far from Nelson school and that there was a church at one end. Now I only had to narrow down which house she lived in and write out a script of what I would say to her when I found her.

"Hello, Sheena Meyer." *No, not that.* "Yo, what up, Sheena?" *Nope.* "Hey, Sheena. It's me, Alaina. You don't know me? That's okay. I need to talk to you about something." *That could work.* Then I could tell her everything and hope she didn't think I was crazy.

"Leif, Leif, Leif . . ."

He groaned.

I shook him. "Wake up. Don't you think we need to go Christmas shopping today?"

He sat up, rubbing his eyes. "You mean at the mall?"

"I mean at the game store."

Leif snapped out of any sleep that was left and hauled out of the room. "Grandma, can we go Christmas shopping today!"

"That was too easy," I mumbled.

Bundled up and headed to Lake Mall, I wondered how far we were from Sheena Meyer's neighborhood.

"Grandma, do we live far from... Uh..." I tried to remember a place I saw on the map. "Muskegon High School?"

"Our neighborhood is really considered part of North Muskegon."

"But isn't the youth center we usually go to when we visit near the high school?"

"It is. That's the one I prefer you attend."

"Soooo . . . Can we drive over that way—I mean to that area so I can remember?"

Grandma Eleanor smirked. "Remember what? How about while we're out, we stop and get you signed up at the center, so you have something to do with the rest of the adults your age."

"We're still going to the mall, right?"

"It's on the way," I told Leif.

Once we drove off the exit from US 31, I read every street sign. Soon we were on Jefferson Street, and I saw the church on the corner. *Oh my gosh, this is it!* That's where we turned right, onto Strong Ave. I was freaking-out inside, feeling like a thousand frogs were jumping around in my stomach. *Yuck why do I think things like that.* The visual grossed me out.

We are driving down Sheena Meyer's street! I yelled inside—*if I had figured out the clues correctly. But which house is it?*

Snow covered everything, but despite the snow, there were kids outside in front of one of the houses.

Leif's eyes closed and he tilted his head left and right as he sang, "Up in the air!"

"Grandma. Grandma, stop singing." She and Leif were now belting out the weird lyrics together.

"What's wrong?"

"Can you turn around? I think I saw one of my friends."

"Did you? Where?"

I pointed behind us. "Back there."

Grandma pulled into the next driveway we came to, backed out, and drove up Strong Avenue in the opposite direction.

Slow down, I told her, looking at the houses.

"Why are you whispering?"

"I don't know."

To the right of us, two girls and a boy were in front of a two-story house. The boy stood with a leg on either side of his bike. *They ride bikes in the snow?* The kids looked to be my age or no more than fourteen.

"Is that them?" asked my grandmother.

"I don't know. Roll down the window a little . . ."

"You're saying you will know it's them if you hear them?"

"Something like that," I replied.

One of the girls had curly hair and wore a heavy coat. The other wore a white coat with white fur around the hood. They were laughing and then the one in white swung her arm at the boy on the bike. "Stop it, Theodore," she exclaimed.

Theodore . . . I made a mental note of his name as the car slowed.

"What are you doing?"

"Allowing you to get a good look so you can say hello."

"No, Grandma, that's not necessary. I can see from here."

She acted like I wasn't even talking and pulled right into the driveway, and I thought I was going to pass out right then and there. It felt like someone had turned the heat up inside the car to two hundred degrees. The frogs were gone from my stomach and replaced with a hole that was sinking into my spine.

No, no, no. This is not happening. I pulled my hat down and the hood of my coat over my head.

Grandma Eleanor put the car in park and, without even asking me, rolled down my window. I was right there, face to face with some random kids I didn't know.

They waited for us to say something.

"My granddaughter is a little shy," she yelled across me. "She thought she knew you from the last time she was in town and wanted to check. That's what you said right?" she asked, looking at me while I gave her my, stop-it-what-are-you-doing look.

I'm so embarrassed, I thought and looked up at them. "I'm sorry. I thought you were someone else."

"Who?" asked the girl in the white coat. We might know them."

Did she seriously ask me that? Think Alaina. Think up a name. "Uh, Corn."

"Corn?" asked the boy, Theodore.

Why did I say that? Hurry, think of something! I blushed. "Short for Cornelia."

"Oh, never heard of her. Hey, she might not be our age. What are you, about ten? Eleven?"

Grandma Eleanor snickered.

"I'm thirteen."

"Chana, you know everybody. Do you know Corn?" asked Theodore. "I know Sheena doesn't."

My eyes widened. *It's her.*

"Teddy, why did you say my name?"

"Teddy?"

"She could be working for the Murk and trying to hunt me down." I think she thought she was whispering, but I could hear every word she said.

"Okay, well . . . Thank you," I told them.

Chana looked at me oddly, took a step closer and stared into my eyes. "Yeah, no problem. Be blessed."

"Be blessed?" Theodore shrieked. "Like you're all holy."

I rolled up my window and Grandma Eleanor shifted the car in reverse so we could back out of the driveway, but the wheels just spun in the snow.

She rolled down her window and poked her head out. "You kids give me a push." She looked over at me. "You too. Get out there."

Double embarrassed.

"And me?" asked Leif.

"No, you stay right where you are."

Theodore, Chana, Sheena, and a tall man with a goatee that came out of the side door of the house joined me, placing their gloved hands on the hood of the car. I braced my feet as best I could as we all pushed, fearing I would slide right under the SUV.

I'm right next to her. Sheena Meyer. The one I'm supposed to help, I thought as I glanced over, wondering why my grandmother even told me to help knowing I had tiny muscles. The SUV rocked back a couple of times, and then it was free and rolling into the street.

Grandma held her hand up and waved, as though yelling, "Thank you!" wasn't enough.

I got into the car and looked back, watching them as we pulled away. And . . . Though Sheena and Theodore went back to what they were doing, Chana never took her eyes off me.

Chapter Eight

The Hackley Youth Center was only a couple of blocks over from Strong Ave. "Those kids we saw didn't know your friend, Corn, but maybe she's here," Grandma Eleanor said as she got out of the car.

I mentally face-palmed. Why did I have to call her Corn?

We walked through the glass doors, and she headed straight to the reception desk, pulled out a pen, and began filling out a form on a clipboard that asked about allergies and emergency contacts.

"Hey, Mrs. Eleanor," said the woman behind the desk.

"Hello Shawna," she replied. Everyone passing through the office knew her, and she greeted them all with a smile and nod.

Shawna clasped her hands together. "Please say you'll bring some of your infamous banana pudding the next time you come."

"I just may be able to arrange that," Grandma Eleanor replied.

I stood beside her, glancing over my shoulder left and right. "Leif?"

Grandma Eleanor spun around. "Where did he go? Go find him."

I sprinted down the long hallway, my wet sneakers squeaking against the linoleum floors. The sound of laughter and the thud of basketballs echoed from the gymnasium. I spotted Leif in the chaotic mix of kids that looked to range in age from seven to my age and older, his coat flying open and him tossing it aside as he chased after a red kickball.

"Leif!" I called out, trying to catch his attention above the noise.

"Does he have to go? They were starting a new game."

I walked over to the girl with a black headband holding back thick crinkly hair that looked freshly unbraided.

"I'm Alaysia," she said. "I'm not playing with them. I'm just watching my brother and sisters."

Kids ran all around us. "All of these are—"

Alaysia laughed. "Not all of them."

She yelled their names. "Anthony, Selah, Sahara, Zariyah! There are two more who aren't here today: Messiah and Naimah."

Her siblings came running. "He's my twin," she said, pushing her brother over by the shoulders.

"Cool."

"We have to go," I told Leif.

"Already?" He picked up his coat.

"We're coming back."

"We're in town until the end of the year," said Alaysia.

"Us too."

"It'll be good to have someone else my age here."

"How old are you," Leif asked her.

"Thirteen."

"She's not your age," said Leif.

I nudged him. "You know good and well I'm thirteen."

"By only a few days."

"Can you not?"

Alaysia laughed. "You never said your name."

"Alaina."

"We have similar names."

"Yeah, we're the A-team." *Why did I say that?*

Grandma Eleanor stood at the gym entrance doors waving us over. "Gotta go. See you guys. Anthony, Selah, Sahara, and Za . . . Zariyah. Did I get all of their names right?"

"Surprisingly," said Alaysia, with a grin. "You have a good memory."

"I try to pay attention. Bye," I said, grabbed Leif's hand, and hurried away.

"Hey, Alaina," yelled Selah. "Alaysia's a bookworm. Do you like to read?"

"Stop telling my business. But I am!"

"I am too." *Sort of.*

"Ooo," she said and ran over. "You should check out the books by Stephen Woodruff—I mean unless you're already reading them. They have some here in the library."

"My grandmother actually has some."

"That gives me an idea." She wrote on a small notebook pad she kept in her pocket and tore the page off. "Here's my email."

She's giving me her email address and not her phone number?

"Email me the titles she has, and we'll read together."

"Yeah, the A-team book club." *Why do I bother to open my mouth?* "See ya. Come on, Leif."

He ignored me and tried to steal the basketball from Alaysia's brother, Anthony, but was doing a terrible job at it. Again, he lunged for the basketball clumsily, his fingers barely grazing its surface. Anthony easily dribbled past him with a grin.

"Bye," Leif said, and we ran over to Grandma Eleanor.

"I see you found your friends."

"Can we come back tomorrow?" asked Leif.

"Tired of me already? I think we can do that. One of us, Mintz or me, will bring you."

"The next stop's the mall," said Leif.

At that point, I wasn't interested in shopping. My mind was on meeting Sheena Meyer. I'd actually found her like the book told me. Now I had to help her. But I couldn't get over her weird friend. The way that girl, Chana, watched me wasn't normal.

Grandma Eleanor bought us boots, and we shopped for gifts for our parents. She allowed Leif to get a gift he could play with right now because he begged. "Please, oh please," he whined and promised never to do this and that again. She might not admit it, but I think Leif was her favorite. She always gave in to him. I was the one she always gave a hard time, while with Leif it was, "Whatever you want my sweet, precious, Leify-Poo."

Unlike other people, Grandma Eleanor didn't celebrate Christmas with gifts. She loved the holiday season and the decorations, but she only gave us gifts because she hardly saw us. She said gifts weren't what Christmas was truly about. I understood, but I was happy about the gifts—and even more about the money she often sent so I could buy what I really wanted or needed myself.

When we got home, we carried our shopping bags inside, and as usual, Mintz had the place warm and toasty, and I realized how hungry I was.

"I'm hungry," said Leif, as if reading my mind. Grandma Eleanor wouldn't let us eat at the mall. "That's how you get food poisoning," she said. I didn't bother telling her we ate at the mall all the time with our mom.

Dinner was a crab boil. My stomach growled as I hungrily eyed the newspaper-lined island covered in a spread of king crab legs, boiled eggs, corn on the cob, and baby potatoes covered in a garlicy sauce. I didn't care about the crab as much as I cared for the eggs, corn, and potatoes.

It was a mess of a dinner, but it was delicious.

Afterward, I helped clean up and turned to leave the kitchen.

"Where are you going?" asked Grandma Eleanor.

"To read," I exclaimed.

"Make sure your hands are clean first! She'd better not get melted butter or sauce on my books, right Leif?"

"Right!" he replied, sucking on a crab leg shell.

I hurried away and closed the door to the library behind me, hoping no one followed me. I listening at the door. When I was certain I was alone, I turned to the book on the table. "I did it," I said aloud. "I found Sheena Meyer."

I waited, not knowing what would happen next. Maybe a voice would say, "Good job" or something. Maybe God would say, "Well done, my good and faithful servant."

The book was closed with the butterfly emblem tempting me to open it. *Why a butterfly,* I wondered.

I heard something behind me and turned.

My body jolted like I had been hit with a surge of electricity. The girl, Sheena Meyer's friend, was standing in the library, staring at me.

I barely had time to scream before she rushed at me, moving faster than any normal person should, and clamped her hand over my mouth, cutting off the sound.

My breathing quickened, my arms were tight to my sides, like Grandma Eleanor's wooden soldier ornaments, and my shoulders rose fast with each breath.

"Calm down," she whispered.

My eyes were wild. Calm down? Was she serious? *What was her name? Chana.*

"Are you calm?" she asked. "I'm not letting go until you are."

I nodded, and she slowly removed her hand from my mouth.

"H-how are you here? W-what do you want?"

"You're here to help Sheena, aren't you?"

I nodded.

She grinned and I stopped shaking. But the way she looked into my eyes creeped me out. "I see you," she said. "Does your family know?"

"Know what?"

She looked up and around the room as if just noticing the shelves of books. "That you're a chrono gleamer. Sheena would love this library."

"A-a w-what?" I stammered.

"Don't tell me you don't know."

Could she not see the shock on my face?

"What is this?" she asked, walking away from me. "The Aetates Papilio?"

I nodded.

"You can read this, can't you?" she asked as if she already knew the answer.

"Uh . . . just like everyone else can."

Her eyes locked on me.

"Everyone else *can*, right?"

"Not exactly. Most can't see the writings at all. But you have the ability to delve into past, present, and future events as they are depicted in this book as it pertains to gleamers—to help them. That's its purpose." She glanced at me and by the expression on my face, I think she realized I didn't understand what she was saying. "This book gives you a special connection to its contents and the events unfolding in both your world and Sheena's."

I sat, dumbfounded. "What are you talking about?"

"You solve mysteries and anticipate future challenges. You've seen it light up, right?"

"Yes."

"That sounds about right. You've turned thirteen and have come of age."

"Because I'm officially a woman now?"

"If you say so," she said, clearly holding back a snicker. "The book is reacting to your presence because it recognizes your gleamer abilities; lighting up and revealing hidden messages or passages that are crucial for your quest."

"My quest?"

"Your mission."

"But that doesn't explain why you are here or how you got here?"

The air around us began to tingle and the hair on my arms stood on end. Chana started to glow, emitting a soft white light that danced and swirled around her, and I got ready to run out of there, but she was blocking the door. In seconds. The glow vanished and she waited. I didn't know what she expected me to say. There was no reason on earth that a kid would start glowing on demand. *On earth...*

"What are you?"

"A heavenly helper."

I gasped. "An angel? Do you mean an angel?"

She looked satisfied.

"You came here to tell me that?"

"I came here because we have a mission."

"We?"

"By New Year's Day."

"But we leave to go back home right past Christmas. How am I supposed to find a reason to stay here after Christmas?"

"That's for you to figure out. But remember, this is not just about helping Sheena. Your actions will impact your future and that of the city and kids everywhere."

I felt weight pressing onto my shoulders as Chana spoke. This was a lot of responsibility for a thirteen-year-old.

"Don't worry. I'm confident you can do it," said Chana. "Have you seen your guardian yet?"

I hopped up from my seat. "My guardian? As in angel? You mean in person?"

"Yes, that's what I meant—not that you have to. I'm just curious. But . . . there's something else out there and I'm just glad I got to you before it did."

"It?"

Chapter Nine

"What do you mean by *it*?" I asked, but I knew exactly what Chana meant. I shuddered and felt the blood drain from my face, remembering the dark encounter when I asked the book what Sheena was in danger from.

"The Murk."

"That's what it's called? So this Murk—it's real?' I asked nervously.

Chana nodded and looked to her right. "I'm afraid so . . . Oh, she saw it already? Did it scare her? Okay."

"Wait . . . Who are you talking to?"

Chana lifted a finger. "Hold on, I'm having a conversation right now with your guardian."

I gasped. "You're talking to my guardian angel? Right now?"

Chana doubled over in laughter. "Gleamers always fall for that. No, I wasn't, but anyway, the Murk is a dark force that has plagued this town and the world for centuries. It manifests as a dense fog or mist that envelops its surroundings, its form constantly shifting, making it difficult to pinpoint or describe accurately."

"That's it. That's what I saw, but why here?"

"That's a long story. But what you need to know right now is that things are escalating because of Sheena. She's special like you, but in a different way, and the Murk knows it."

"Are you saying it knows about me?"

"Possibly. Probably. You got any black licorice?"

"Yuck and no."

"The Murk is gaining power from the same kids that can kill it. It hates kids."

"Why?"

"Because you hold the hope of the world. Even more than adults. That hope can kill it. It would rather you be angry, terrified, and filled with fear. Those things strengthen it and kill you. It preys on the fears and vulnerabilities of its targets. It thrives on chaos and confusion, enjoying the torment it brings to others."

"So gleamers—"

"With the help of angels, help to save our youth and the world. Without gleamers the world is defenseless. The Murk knows this. It wants to snuff out their light, one by one. Or absorb it to make itself more powerful," Chana said and turned like she was going to walk out of the library.

"Hey, where are you going? I have no idea what I'm supposed to do now."

She pointed at the bookshelves. "Maybe you should sit and do a little reading."

In the blink of an eye she was gone, and I looked behind every piece of furniture in the room like she might be hiding there.

That really happened. I need to call Penelope. I need to—oh yeah, "Stephen Woodruff, the author Alaysia mentioned." I went to the bookshelves to the left of the entrance. I knew I read his name on the spine of a few books over there. *There's one.* I pulled the book from the shelf. *Knight of the Day* was the title, in gold metallic, with a tiny dragon under it. I ran from the library. "Grandma, I need to use your laptop."

"I don't have a laptop," she yelled from somewhere in the house.

"Then your tablet," I yelled as I ran through the kitchen looking for her.

"I don't have a tablet."

Oh my gosh, she's stuck in 1980 or something. I found her in her office. "Then what do you use?"

"Do you not see this desktop?"

"Yes, but the monitor is so big. That's all you use?"

"Do you want to use it or not?"

"Yes. I met Alaysia at the center, and she told me to email the titles of Stephen Woodruff's books you have because she's reading his books."

"Stephen Woodruff's books aren't exactly middle grade."

"I read young adult—"

She held her hand up. "And before you give me the whole 'I'm almost an adult' speech, I've read them, so I know they are appropriate for an advanced reader like yourself." She rose from the computer, and I sat in her desk chair. "Do you know how to use this?"

"Yes." I looked over my shoulder. "You're not going to give me any privacy?"

She placed a hand on her hip. "In my office? At my computer? I don't think so."

I emailed Alaysia as Grandma Eleanor watched, and then we left the office together. "Where is Leif?" I asked.

"I don't know. Why don't you go and find him? But leave that," she said, pointing at the book under my arm, "in the library, or sign it out using one of the cards on the wall beside the door."

"Sign it out?"

"That's what I said."

I rolled my eyes but did as Grandma Eleanor asked, signing out the Stephen Woodruff book on one of her old-fashioned library cards before going to hunt down Leif. Passing a window, I saw something laying on the ground. Then it moved. I got my coat and went outside. Leif lay on his back in the snow, gazing up at the clouds drifting by overhead.

"Whatcha doing out here?" I asked, plopping down on the ground beside him.

Leif looked over at me, his eyes bright. "Just making snow angels and cloud watching. That one looks like a dragon." He pointed to a puffy white and gray cloud.

I nodded, following his finger. "Yeah, I can see that." We were quiet, watching the shapes shift and morph in the sky. I breathed in the fresh air and closed my eyes. "It's so quiet here. No cars honking or sirens blaring."

Suddenly, Leif sat upright, eyes wide. "Did you feel that?"

"'Feel what?" I asked, startled.

"I don't know . . . it was like a ripple in the air, or something." Leif furrowed his brow. "Energy."

I stared at my little brother. "I didn't feel anything. Are you sure you're not just imagining things?"

"I'm telling you, there was something . . ." Leif trailed off, glancing around uneasily.

Leif was usually just a happy kid without a care in the world, so seeing him like this bothered me. A chill ran down my spine, adding to the cold that already gripped me. What had Leif sensed? I didn't know, and while I didn't want to encourage his suspicions, I couldn't shake the uneasy feeling creeping over me. It felt like... we were being watched.

The next morning, Grandma Eleanor drove us over to the youth center, signed us in, and before she left for work, said, "Do it."

"Grandma, no. Not in here. It's bad enough you make me do it when we're outside somewhere."

"Alaina . . ." she said, tilting her head and raising a brow with that look—the one that said she expected to be obeyed, like a queen who is never challenged and always gets her way.

"My Grandmother is the most incredible human in the world," I yelled. *I'm so embarrassed.*

"Aww sweetie, thank you," Grandma Eleanor said and lowered her voice. "That's for making me late. Bye-bye."

She left me standing there, and I hated to have to turn around and see who had witnessed all of that. But I did, and there was Shawna, grinning at her computer. "You guys can head down to the gym until the sessions begin," she said.

"Thanks," I replied. "Come on, Leif."

I trudged down the hall and stepped through the double doors of the gym. Leif grabbed my hand and squeezed it tightly. No one was playing yet. They stood around talking. Maybe it was too early and their morning adrenaline hadn't kicked in. We scanned the room and stood close together, waiting for the other kids to speak to us rather than stare.

"Hey," came from behind us.

I turned, seeing Sahara. At least I thought she was Sahara. She could've been Selah. They wore similar braided hairstyles, but her braids had beads on the ends and I think Selah was taller. After I got to know them better, I would know which was which.

"She came back," she yelled over her shoulder. Her siblings hurried inside, and Leif followed Anthony around the gym as if he was his hero.

"I got your email," said Alaysia. "You don't know how much it means to be able to discuss Stephen Woodruff's books with someone. Okay, I have so many theories, but tell me, what do you think about—"

"You can't just hit her with all of that as soon as you see her," said Selah. "She's just trying to impress you," she whispered.

"No, I'm not."

"Yes, you are."

"I'm literally impressive. I mean, do you not know me?"

I liked Alaysia. She was pretty smart. I could tell. Not nerd smart, although that's not a bad thing, but like a person who knew things and caught onto things easily. Like . . . Like a mom. She was an adult in a kid's body. Maybe having so many siblings younger than her helped with that.

Another thing I noticed was that Alaysia and her siblings had the brightest smiles, as if they didn't know how boring or underwhelming the world could be.

"Here he comes," said Selah, nudging Sahara.

"Who?" I asked.

"Hurry, walk this way."

I didn't know which way she meant so I about-faced. *WHAM!* I walked right into a boy. His forehead collided with my nose.

"Oww," he exclaimed.

I barely even felt the impact, but I was stunned for a moment. Forget Noah, this was the most perfect boy I had ever seen. He had eyes that said, "Hello Alaina," a nose that made you care about noses, and lips that . . . well, his lips were chapped, but still... It didn't even matter that he was shorter than me. He had perfect skin, and his hair looked like it had just been lined up at the barber.

In my attempt to get away from him I shuffled back and forth. He did the same, trying to get around me, and I stepped on his foot.

"Oww," he exclaimed, again.

Then it happened. I watched it in slow motion. A lone drop of blood drifted down onto his white shoe.

He screamed.

My hand clasped over my nose, and Alaysia grabbed me. "Peroxide," she said, pointed at his shoe, and then whisked me away. "Anthony watch Leif!"

"Got 'em!" he yelled back.

Whispers and giggles came from a few kids in the youth center as we passed by, and my face flushed red with embarrassment. This was not the impression I hoped to make on my first day at the center or with my first interaction with a cute boy. *A nosebleed? Why did we have to run into each other?*

Alaysia pushed open the door to the bathroom and led me over to the sink where she looked at me apologetically before gently holding a tissue to my nose.

"I am so sorry," I mumbled, pulling the tissue away from my face to see if the bleeding had lessened.

"It's okay, really," Alaysia reassured me with a smile. "It happens all the time here. It's part of the chaos that comes with a room full of energetic kids."

"What? Butting heads and getting nosebleeds? Do you know him?" I asked, nodding towards the hall.

"Yeah, that's Patrick," Alaysia said with a grin, as if his name alone should explain everything.

"Patrick..." I repeated his name silently to myself, liking how it rolled off my tongue.

Alaysia giggled. "Uh-oh . . . we've got another one."

"What's that supposed to mean?"

"He's pretty popular around here," Alaysia grabbed more tissue. "He's been coming here for a couple of years now."

"Oh, we didn't come to Muskegon last year."

"See what you missed. I mean all any girl ever does is stare at him." She dabbed at my nose again and handed me the tissue.

"Looks like it stopped. Just make sure there's no dried blood left on there."

I looked up my nostrils while I washed my hands. *Might as well check for boogers while I'm at it.* Other than my nose being a little red, I was fine. My two French braids weren't frizzy or anything, despite my hat. I looked okay.

"Come on," she said, grabbing my hand and leading me back to the gym. "Let's introduce you properly."

I followed her apprehensively, not wanting to embarrass myself any further in front of Patrick or anyone else for that matter. But as we approached him and his group of friends, something strange happened.

The chatter and laughter faded around us, and the other kids seemed to fall away until it was just Patrick standing there alone, staring at me intently. His piercing brown eyes locked onto mine, and I felt a sudden swooping sensation in my stomach, like I was free-falling through the air.

"Hey, sorry about that," he said sincerely. "I'm Patrick," he added. "I should've been looking where I was going. My dad says I never do."

I was so surprised by his apology that I just stood there with my mouth open. "Alaina," I managed to squeak out finally, feeling like an invisible hand was squeezing my lungs. I blushed again. "No, it was totally my fault. Sorry about head-butting you. I can be kind of clumsy sometimes."

Off to the side, his friends elbowed each other and snickered.

"Don't worry about it. I've had worse on the basketball court. At least you didn't give me a bloody nose too."

"Yeah . . . " I looked down. The spot was gone from his shoe.

He noticed my expression. "Alaysia was right. The peroxide worked. They had some in the office. No harm done."

He pointed at the kids near us. "This is Tony, José, and Brady. Guys, this is Alaina."

"And I'm Leif!" my brother piped up, dribbling a basketball over to me.

"Hey, pass it here," said Brady.

"You have to catch me first." Leif dribbled away and accidentally kicked the ball, sending the boys running after it.

Patrick grinned and leaned in conspiratorially. "So, welcome to the winter break club, you're officially one of us now that you've survived an encounter with my thick skull."

Is he being cute? No, that was a joke. "Ha!" I exclaimed. *That was too delayed. I'm so weird.*

"Come on," Alaysia said, pulling me. If you're not going to eat breakfast, we can go to class."

"They serve breakfast here?"

"Yeah, in the cafeteria," said a boy in passing. He frowned, as if my question made him instantly hate me.

"Oh, okay . . ." I replied.

"Ignore him," said a girl with her hair pulled up into afro puffs down the center of her head like a mohawk. I guess I wasn't the only one who noticed his attitude.

"Whatever, Quincy," the boy muttered, rolling his eyes and pulling the hood of his jacket over his head.

"Says the guy who wants you to be more pacific," Quincy shot back. "I'm Quincy," she said, glancing over at me. "Or Quinn. Whichever." She turned back. "The word is specific, Sir Ballard. The Pacific is an ocean!"

"That was a year ago." His face turning red as he stormed off. "And stop using my full name," he yelled over his shoulder.

Quincy giggled. "No joke. That's his real name. He hates it. Especially when you say the whole thing."

"So his first name is Sir?" I asked.

Quincy nodded. "Sir Ballard!" she called.

"Stop it," said Alaysia. "He's already in a bad mood. You're just making it worse."

"He'll be all right. I'm going to breakfast. Who are you?"

"Oh, I'm Alaina."

"Ooo, oh, nose-bleed girl!" she exclaimed as if she were excited to meet me. "Don't be ashamed of that. Are you coming to breakfast?"

"No, I'm not hungry." I'm sure everyone would love to see the "nose-bleed" girl joining them.

"Okay, see you guys later."

We watched Quincy walk away. She naturally had a style about her, and I wondered what it was like to be her. Outspoken, confident, a funky style and just, well . . . herself.

"I think she likes him," Alaysia whispered.

"I don't think so," said her sister, Selah. "He's one of the mean ones."

"Mean ones?"

"Yeah. They're mean to people for no reason at all. They stick together too."

"Do they bother you?" I asked.

"Nope, because if they mess with one of us, they have to deal with all of my siblings. Just ignore them or tell one of the instructors if they bother you," said Alaysia.

I thought all I had to worry about was this Murk thing. Now I had mean kids. Great.

Chapter Ten

"What's in here?" I asked about the room Alaysia was leading me to.

"You'll see."

We stepped inside. The walls were painted in abstract waving patterns, in shades of teal, yellow, orange, and green. Above those was a quote: *Creativity is the spark that turns dreams into reality.* Artwork created by the kids covered the lower walls.

I walked along shelves with various supplies: bins filled with colored paper, beads, ribbons, fabric scraps, and paints in every shade imaginable. In the center of the room was a long, sturdy table dotted with remnants of past projects: splashes of paint, bits of glitter, and old glue.

"Any minute and Mrs. Perry is going to come in full of holiday cheer and try to get you to make a beaded friendship bracelet, you probably made in third grade, to give to someone for Christmas," said Alaysia.

I shrugged. "I like bracelets."

"Bracelets are cool unless you have too many, but let's talk about the book. What do you think?"

"I'm not really into castles and kings and dragons and stuff, but I think it's a good story. The pace is good."

Alaysia stared at me.

"What?"

"You haven't noticed anything?" she asked.

"Anything like what?"

"The correlation between Muskegon and that book—all of Stephen Woodruff's books."

My eyes bulged. "There's a dragon here?"

Alaysia fell into Selah, laughing. "No." She composed herself, wiping tears from her eyes. "There are no dragons in Muskegon that I know of," she said, catching her breath.

I stared at Alaysia, puzzled. "Then what did you mean about the book and Muskegon?"

Alaysia became more serious and leaned in, lowering her voice. "Haven't you noticed the strange things happening in this town? I've seen...stuff. At first, I thought I was going crazy, and even my own siblings don't believe me," she said, giving Selah the side eye.

"Proof. That's all I'm saying," said Selah. "I need proof."

Alaysia turned back to me. "Yeah, anyway, like I was saying. I thought I was nuts but then—"

She stopped abruptly, seeing Mrs. Perry breeze in wearing all black, looking like she was about to hit the slopes with her skis. She held an armful of beading supplies.

"Happy holidays to you, and you, and you," she sang with a smile as she pointed at us. "All right kids, who's ready to make some bracelets?"

"Told you."

Alaysia introduced me to Mrs. Perry. Other kids hurried into the room, and we got started—about twelve of us in all.

I mechanically strung beads onto a cord, listening and not listening to the conversations around me at the same time. Maybe I hadn't read enough of Stephen Woodruff's books to notice the similarities that Alaysia talked about. Or maybe she imagined it all. But was I imagining what I saw in Grandma Eleanor's library, and did I imagine Chana appearing there and being some kind of angel? Maybe I hallucinated. The fumes from all the old books could have affected my brain or something.

"Huh?" I looked around, certain someone had said my name.

"I *said*, what brought you to Muskegon?" a younger boy, with curly hair and glasses, across from me asked.

"Oh, we're in town for the holidays." I replied, stringing a blue bead onto my bracelet. "I'm from North Carolina."

"Your grandmother? Is that who you are visiting?"

"Why are you interrogating her, Deuce? You're so nosy," said Selah.

"It's okay. Yes," I replied.

"What about before North Carolina? Were you from around here?" He pressed on.

Now it wasn't okay. I hesitated before answering. I didn't understand his questioning. Did he really need to know if I was originally from Muskegon?

Alaysia seemed to sense my discomfort and quickly changed the subject, but the boy kept glancing over at me.

The session ended with us examining each other's work. I mean they were beads, so there wasn't going to be huge differences when we were all using the same beads. But Alaysia had added a letter bead every few beads between the others.

"It's my mom's name," she explained.

"Write your name on this tag and tie it to your bracelet," said Mrs. Perry. "You can come back and get them later."

We hung them on hooks on the back wall and Alaysia led me down the hall. "We can take a tour between sessions. Everyone meets back up in the gym."

"Remember, I've been here before."

"Yeah, but you haven't seen all the updates."

In one room, kids were dancing behind an instructor facing a mirrored wall, watching themselves, as the words of the hip hop song repeated over a fast beat, "When I get'cha...When

I get'cha...." They skipped to the side twice and spun. The instructor cheered them on for getting the routine down.

Alaysia pulled me. "Come on."

The next room was larger. Patrick ran, took a light-footed leap and then slid under a bar.

"This is like a huge jungle gym. You're right. They *have* made a lot of changes here."

"Yeah, this place has gone through a whole remodel. I heard someone donated the money for the updates."

Patrick grabbed Tony and he stomped away, disappointed.

"Are they playing tag?"

Alaysia nodded. "Kind of. It's chase tag—parkour involving tag."

"That's a thing?"

"Yes! They even have a world championship. I didn't know about it either until last year."

Her sister, Selah, pointed high up on the wall at the letters. "There is also a deeper meaning."

Talents

Abilities

Gifts

"Oh, gotcha."

Patrick and Tony brought Leif over, laughing. "No one can catch him," said Tony.

Patrick nodded. "We need him on the team. He's a natural."

"I'm a pro," said Leif.

"We're not in town long enough for that."

"Gotcha," said a girl grabbing Patrick around the waist."

"I called a time out," he replied, laughing at her.

"Chana?" I said, as she pulled her braids out of her face and tucked them securely in one of her two ponytail bands.

"The one and only."

"You know each other?" asked Alaysia.

"We just met the other day," Chana replied for me. She was sweating like a human being.

"Chana is here all the time."

"I like this place. And I bring joy to the kids who have to be here over break. Consider this my way of giving back to the community."

I nodded, not understanding why she would be there, as if she were actually human, living a life on earth—but she kind of was.

As we settled into our chairs for our next session, a student helper walked around with a tray of juice boxes, while another came by with a wicker basket filled with individually wrapped snacks.

"What's wrong?" asked Sahara, seeing my expression.

I hesitated before shaking my head at the basket. "I don't eat processed foods," I explained.

She raised an eyebrow in surprise. "Ever?"

"Rarely."

"You'll probably starve here," said Alaysia.

The lady in charge heard us. "Don't say that. There is fresh fruit over here and bottled water. You can also bring your own next time."

"Thanks," I replied.

"You've got your snacks. Good." said the male instructor who walked in. "When you're done, we're going to have some fun. You're going to love it. I thought of everyone." He set a bin of white plastic balls in front of us. "We're making ornaments."

We all just watched him.

"Calm down. You all are getting a little too excited about this."

I giggled, and he pointed at me. "I made you laugh," he said and motioned at a shelf. "We have lots of paint. Careful with the glitter please. You can use these as gifts, stocking stuffers, or hang them on your tree. Create ornaments that reflect your culture and the spirit of the season."

"What about Justina," asked Alaysia.

"I'm making a menorah."

"See? Did I not say I thought of everyone?"

An hour later, with our ornaments drying and our stomachs growling, we headed to lunch and after that, about half of the kids left, including Quincy, leaving only a few of us for the afternoon activities.

Chana gestured with her head, and I moved closer as she grabbed her coat. She lowered her voice. "Don't be fooled by appearances. Things that seem good may not be, and things that seem perfect, rarely are. Stay on guard."

What was that supposed to mean? I nodded as if I understood. Could she be talking about a person?

Chana shook her head. "You know how you get that feeling that someone is behind you, but you turn, and you don't see anyone?"

"Yeah..."

"Don't dismiss that feeling. There is something there. But you have to determine if it is friend, like your guardian, or foe. If you don't have a good feeling... Run."

Chapter Eleven

I stared at Chana, trying to understand. What did she mean by "foe?" I was in a happy place today and she was spoiling it. Her presence alone confused me. I needed to hear her say it. *What foe?*

Before I could ask for clarification, Chana slipped away, disappearing into the crowd of parents checking out their kids. I looked through them, hoping to spot her braided ponytails, but she was nowhere to be seen.

"You okay?" asked Alaysia, noticing the confused look on my face.

"Yeah, I'm fine," I replied absently.

"Let's go to the library."

"Okay."

The library hadn't changed much. It was still part of the same classroom it had been in the last time I came. But there were a ton of new donated books.

"Here," said Alaysia, setting a book on the table between us. "This is the Stephen Woodruff book you have at home, right?"

"Yep, that's it."

She turned the pages. "This book says something is going to happen." She read: "A city destroyed. Hope lost."

"I didn't get to that part yet."

"Well, it's talking about Muskegon."

"Wasn't this book written years ago?" I flipped to the copyright page while holding her page with my finger. "1982. That's like, ancient."

She nodded matter-of-factly. "I knew you would say that." She turned the page and pointed at the words as she read. "Many moons from now, in the year when the clock counts to the four-and-twentieth hour and the people walk with glass in hand, the shadow will rise over the city on the harbor of a lake that is as wide as an ocean. The dragons of old stir once more, not in the lands of yore, but in the streets you now tread. The iron beasts that hum with power shall be no match for the darkness that creeps, for it is not bound by the years it once knew but seeks to claim *the time of now*."

"Yore?" I asked.

"That means long ago, I already Googled it. And the glass in hand and iron beasts represent smartphones and cars. You see it? You *do* see it right? Don't tell me you can't see it."

Alaysia's eyes anticipated my "Heck yeah. I see it, girl!" But I didn't see it. Why would "glass in hand" mean phones instead of goblets? And, for that matter, why would Stephen Woodruff write about people walking around with smartphones years before they even existed? I mean, he couldn't predict the future . . . *could he*? So instead of agreeing, I said, "So this darkness . . . that's what we are concerned about?"

She nodded. She was serious, and I couldn't say she was wrong about that part, based on what I knew.

"Of all the people, why are you sharing this with me? I mean, I'm a stranger. You don't know me from boo."

"I can't explain it. There's something about you. I kind of thought you could help me figure out the meaning of the text."

"And do what about it?"

"Stop it from happening."

"Me and you?"

"No. We could tell the people who can do something."

"Who? The cops? You think they're going to believe a couple of kids? Who in their right mind would believe anything we said about a dark force attacking the city. The Murk is—" *Oops!* My jaws clamped shut and my eyes widened. *Why did I say that?*

"Alaina . . . What are you talking about? I didn't say anything about a Murk." She looked at the doorway and around us before moving closer. "What dark force attacking the city? You know something about what's going on around here, don't you? What do you know?"

My mouth dropped. My mind went blank. What was I going to say? I sat there looking like a mime. I couldn't explain the whole gleam thing and definitely not Grandma Eleanor's book, which I didn't think anyone was supposed to know about.

Before I could make up something to tell her, a scream came from outside. We glanced at each other and ran to the windows. My heart lurched as I spotted Alaysia's sister, Sahara, sprawled at the base of a slide on the playground, clutching her ankle.

Alaysia gasped. "Why is she out there? My mom is going to kill me if she is hurt. I'm supposed to be looking after everyone."

We grabbed our coats and raced to the back door and outside, dropping down beside Sahara.

"What happened?" I asked, gently touching her leg.

Sahara winced, tears filling her eyes. "I slipped on some ice."

"You shouldn't even be out here!" Alaysia fussed.

"They said we could go outside."

I looked around us at the fenced in yard and the sleds beyond it. Other kids watched us with Sahara like it was the most exciting scene they had witnessed all day. Then a woman came through the back door. Sahara groaned, drawing my attention back to her.

I squeezed her hand reassuringly. "Don't worry. Let's get you inside."

With effort, we helped Sahara to her feet, trying not to slip on the ice ourselves. "I've got her," said the woman who came out.

"No, we've got her. She's *my* sister," said Alaysia.

"All right, but be careful. Everyone inside!" the woman yelled. "We have to file an incident report, so take her straight to the office."

Sahara placed an arm around each of us and leaned heavily against me as we slowly made our way back to the youth center. All the while, I couldn't shake the feeling that we were being watched.

Inside, everyone dispersed.

Alaysia and I helped Sahara to the office, where a nurse was on staff. But as she took off her boots and pulled down her sock, I backed away into the hall. I didn't like the sight of blood.

Classes were in session, and I was curious about what each was doing, so I wandered through the building, glancing into each room as I passed. The room closest to the back door was empty. I stepped inside and walked over to the window. A sudden chill made me shiver, as that feeling of being watched still clung to me.

"Hey, do you want to see something cool?"

I glanced behind me. Deuce, the boy with the glasses from the beading class stood at the door to the classroom, looking mischievous.

"Maybe later," I replied and turned back. There was nothing outside but snow, the playground equipment, and the neighborhood houses beyond the field.

"You sure?"

I nodded without turning around, but something caught my eye—a shadow darting past my peripheral vision, disappearing as quickly as it came. I whipped my head around, scanning the empty room. "Deuce?" He was gone also, as if he had never been there. *Did he get mad because I didn't want to see whatever the cool thing was that he wanted to show me? He couldn't move that fast. Could he?* The hair on my arms stood on end. Had that been the "something" Chana warned me about? A foe, not a friend?

I laughed at myself. *I'm just seeing things. This is real life, not some fantasy or horror story.* I headed out of the classroom, but as I stepped into the hallway, I glanced at the back door, and my stomach dropped.

A dark, wispy fog flowed all around the cracks of the door, pooling into the hall. *You're imagining it, Alaina. You're not really seeing this,* I told myself. *Wait, I could be seeing the smoke from someting on fire outside. Yeah, that's it.* But the smoke swirled up from the ground, creeping towards me, deliberate, like something alive. I wanted to scream but I couldn't make a sound and stumbled back.

The fog coiled and twisted, slowly taking form.

I froze, watching it rising and unfurling into the shape of a figure. My legs felt like lead, as I tried to get them to move. And just as its smoky tendrils stretched toward me, a hand grabbed mine and pulled me out of my paralyzed state.

"Run!" was all I heard.

Chapter Twelve

Alaysia and I burst through a set of double doors into the gymnasium. Several youth basketball training sessions were in progress. The thump of the dribbled balls, and the squeak of sneakers on hardwood, echoed through the large room.

"Can you teach me how to dribble the ball between my legs like that?" I heard Leif asking someone as Alaysia whisked me over to the wall.

She stepped in front of me, blocking my view of the room. Her eyes darted around us before landing on me. "I don't know what just happened out there, but I believe you saw something. You stared at the back door for so long, not moving. Did you see something?"

I nodded fast.

"Did it follow us?"

"I-I don't know. Is Sahara okay?"

"Yeah, she was just acting. Drama queen. She didn't even need a bandage."

"Bring your brother and sisters here. I'll get Leif."

She nodded and we spread out, gathering them from around the gym. I didn't know why I told her to do that. It just came out.

They ran up to me, and I held Leif by the hand. Sahara limped.

Alaysia's eyes were wide. "What now? Is it still here?"

"I don't know."

"What's here?" asked Selah.

"You acted afraid. It knows you can see it. That's not good," said Alaysia. "I read something like that in Stephen Woodruff's book. The princess—"

"Not now," I said. I hated to cut her off, but this was no time for a whole synopsis. She was unbelievable. And I meant that in a good way. She actually believed me. "We need to get out of here."

"I know somewhere we can go. Follow me," said Anthony, Alaysia's twin.

We all turned to leave the gym.

"No, not everyone at the same time. Mr. Franklin will notice."

One by one we found our way to the door and then skirted out as if going to the restroom.

Once we were all in the hallway, Anthony waved for us to follow him. "Where are we going?" I asked.

"Just come on."

We followed him through a utility door with a sign that read: STAFF ONLY.

"I don't think we are supposed to be in here," I said as we climbed the stairs beyond the door.

"This is the old part of the building that they don't use anymore," said Anthony.

"Why is it unlocked?"

"I don't know."

"Then how do you know about it?"

"Because I like to explore."

"Just like me," said Leif.

We went into a room filled with old classroom furniture, folding tables, and lots of file boxes. Dust covered everything.

"If something is wrong, why don't we just leave the center?" asked Selah.

"Because we can't get out of here without being signed out by a parent," said Alaysia.

I looked around the room and up at the ceiling. "It's coming…" I told them. I didn't know how I knew, but I knew.

"What's coming?" asked Anthony.

Everyone jumped, hearing the door slam shut.

Sahara backed up, her limp gone. "I don't like this. What is happening?"

"What do you want from me?" I screamed.

"Fear," I heard in a whisper.

"Whatever it is, don't give it what it wants," yelled Alaysia. "We need another way out."

I rushed to one of the tall windows, hoping for an escape route. The glass was cold and fogged up, and the frame was warped. I tried to lift it, but the window was stuck—sealed tight by layers of paint and possibly frost. Using all my strength and a loud groan, I pushed. Anthony hurried over to help, and together, with a forceful shove, the window creaked open just enough to let in a blast of icy air.

We pushed it higher, and I leaned out, gripping the window sill tightly. "That's the roof of the first floor. It's not that far below us," I said, my breath forming a mist in the air. "We can make it."

Anthony glanced out too. "What exactly are we running from?" he asked again.

"Trust me, you don't want to find out," I replied, turning to his sisters. "We can—" A shriek cut through the air behind me. I froze, my heart hammering in my chest. Before I could react, something grabbed me, and I screamed.

Anthony fell off to the side, "What was that?"

The force yanked me backward. My feet lifted off the floor, and I clung desperately to the frame as something tried to pull me out of the window.

"Alaina!" Selah screamed. She grabbed my legs, anchoring me in place. "Alaysia! Help!"

Alaysia wrapped her arms around Selah's waist, both of them straining to pull me back inside. My hands started to slip from the cold window casing, and the invisible force gripped tighter.

"We're being pulled forward! Help!" Alaysia cried.

"Hold on!" Sahara yelled, rushing over. She locked onto Alaysia, while Anthony grabbed Sahara.

"I've got you!" he yelled, as Leif joined the chain, clutching Anthony's shirt, gritting his teeth as he pulled with all his might.

"Don't let me go," I screamed, as my hands tore from the frame.

"We've got you!" Alaysia shouted back.

For a moment, the pull was relentless, dragging me further outside. My upper body dangled out the window, leaving me nearly horizontal, suspended between the freezing air outside and the frantic tugging of my friends. I could only see Selah and Alaysia's faces. They twisted, brows furrowed, and jaws clenched tight, as they strained to pull me back inside. Leif stood on the outside of Anthony, pulling, and for a split second, a glow came from his hands. "Let my sister go," he yelled.

Then, suddenly, the pull weakened and something shoved us forward. My body plunged back inside, and we tumbled, collapsing in a heap on top of Anthony and Leif, breathless and stunned.

"We did it," said Alaysia.

"What just happened?" asked Anthony. "Leif, you said 'let my sister go.' Who were you talking to?"

"I don't know. Get off me," he groaned.

A shrieking roar came from outside the door, and we crowded in, holding onto each other. "You-you guys heard that too?" I asked.

We backed up to the wall beside the open window. And just when I thought whatever was after us was going to come into the room and eat us, Mintz walked in. "What are you doing up here?" she asked in the professional, void of emotion, way she has. "Your instructors are downstairs looking for you. Out! All of you."

"Hey," said Deuce, sticking his head in the door with a wave.

"I found him wandering around the hall up here. You get downstairs too," she told him.

I blinked in confusion as the other kids hurried past Mintz without a word, down the stairs, and out of the door leading to the stairwell we weren't supposed to be using.

I turned to say something to Alaysia, but Mintz ushered my brother and me to our coats. "It's time to go."

I waved goodbye to Alaysia and her siblings as Mintz led us out of the building. My stomach did flips, and I pressed my hand against it, hoping to calm my nerves. What were

Alaysia and her siblings thinking now that I was gone? Were they scared—not just about what happened, but of me?

I stared out the window of Mintz's Bronco as it rumbled down the snowy road away from the youth center. Instead of sitting in the front seat with her, I sat in the back seat beside Leif. Not just because my brother might need me after what he had just experienced, but because I hadn't forgotten about Chana's warning.

I shuddered, pulling my coat tighter around me.

"Are you okay?" asked Leif. He studied me with concern in his bright brown eyes.

"Yeah, I'm fine." I tried to sound convincing. "Just . . . a lot happened today."

Leif nodded. "Sure did. This place is weird."

Mintz's eyes met mine for a moment in the rearview mirror.

"But kind of cool too!" Leif grinned, his fear already forgotten.

But . . . I didn't really notice he was afraid. *I* was. I gasped inside realizing I gave that thing what it wanted. Fear.

I wished I could brush things off so easily as Leif. But I knew more about what was happening based on what Chana told me and what the Aetates Papilio showed me. This was only the beginning.

Half an hour later, the car was quiet as we pulled into Grandma Eleanor's driveway. Mintz didn't play any music for the whole ride and Leif had drifted off. *Who could sleep at a time like this?*

I shook him. "Leif, wake up. We're back."

He looked up at the house and got out on my side of the car. I immediately felt safe as Mintz let us in and we stood in the foyer taking off our shoes and coats. I was so relieved to be back at Shiloh. In my mind, whatever that thing was didn't matter because my grandmother was a superhero and could handle anything.

Grandma Eleanor greeted us with a grin. "How was your day? Whew, get a whiff of you. You smell like you've been in football practice with the Detroit Lions and then ran through a fire."

"I'm starving," said Leif, which he said about five times a day, every day.

"Dinner isn't ready yet. Go and get a snack."

Leif ran off to the kitchen.

"Eleanor. . ." Mintz said, lowering her voice. "It knows about them."

Chapter Thirteen

"How?" The shock was in Grandma Eleanor's expression and her voice. My grandmother, typically so boisterous and full of life, fell eerily silent, her eyes darting between Mintz and me.

Mintz's slender figure stood with her gaze locked on me, her expression unreadable. Her lips parted slightly, but instead of speaking further about what she meant, she dismissed herself.

Grandma Eleanor approached me sternly, making me feel shorter than I already was. "Answer me and do not lie. Something came after you today?"

I nodded fast.

"You've seen it before?"

"Yes," I admitted.

"When?"

"The book showed it to me," I practically whispered.

I shifted uncomfortably under my grandmother's gaze and noticed the faintest light flicker deep in her wise eyes. *What is that?*

"The book." Grandma Eleanor repeated. "What book?"

I hesitated before pointing behind her. "In your library."

Grandma Eleanor inhaled sharply. "Did this book have a symbol on the cover?"

I nodded, a knot of anxiety tightening in my stomach. "A butterfly."

"If she saw it, it saw her too. It knows," said Mintz, reappearing and then leaving again. I think she was on the other side of the wall, listening.

"Oh my," Grandma Eleanor murmured, not really talking to me, but to herself. "I mean, I knew. It was really a test. But I had to find out for sure. When I looked into your eyes—" She abruptly stopped and drew me close.

"Grandma, I don't understand." The strange events of the day replayed in my mind as if I were tallying them to win a prize: the eerie mist, the unseen force, the shrieking roar.

My grandmother gently pulled away and studied my face, her expression softening. "You don't understand? I think you do. You're very perceptive. But there are indeed secrets in this world—families—in this town, going back generations." She walked away and I followed her into the living room. She gestured for me to join her in front of the fireplace.

"You may not have believed this had I told you this before, but I'm sure you'll believe it now. There are things beyond the physical world, forces both good and evil, that have always been at work in Muskegon. Your gift has opened your eyes to them."

"My gift?" No, a gift was some kind of talent or special ability. This wasn't the type of gift I wanted. It definitely wasn't on my wish list. A problem-solving genius or maybe a supercharged intuition—now that would've been cool. But nope, I get gleamer instead.

"Yes, your gift. Though at times it may feel like a burden." She leaned forward and took my hands in hers. "Muskegon has always attracted . . . unusual forces. Forces such as you have seen."

I shivered. "What does it want?"

"Oh, I think you're aware of that already, but I'll add to what you know: to sow fear and chaos, as it always has. But there are those who stand against it, protectors who have kept it at bay. They have long guarded special children like you, who see what others can't."

I sat very still, letting my grandmother's words sink in. Grandma Eleanor was quiet, but she never looked away from me, as though she could see my thoughts. If she could, she would have known that inside I was shouting, "I want out of this nightmare!"

"What has your mother told you of heaven?" she asked.

"I don't know. She never talks about it."

Her brows rose. "She doesn't?"

"No. I mean, we go to church, but we don't really talk about things at home other than saying grace before we eat and prayers before bed."

"So you believe?"

"Yeah, I guess."

"Angels watch over you, Alaina. You can't see them, but they do. What if I told you there are those who can communicate with them?"

"Gleamers?"

She grinned. "What else do you know?"

Wait, did that just mean what she saw when I was four years old was real—her finding me singing with angels?

"I know that everyone in the city is in danger and that I need to help . . . Sheena Meyer."

Grandma Eleanor sat erect. "That's serious." She didn't sound very worried though, so I tried not to show my panic.

"What do I do?"

"There is only one way gleamers get most of their answers. Prayer."

I bowed my head. I wasn't sure how much it would help. I had prayed before for Hannah Levin to have a nosebleed during her Bat Mitzvah while she read from the Torah, because she tripped me in the hall at school. It didn't happen, but that worked out because we're friends now. And I would have felt terrible for that to happen to my girl.

Grandma Eleanor chuckled, and I opened one eye and looked up at her. "I didn't mean right now," she said.

"Oh, weren't you about to pray for me? Us?"

"No. I will, and I do, but this prayer must come from you." She leaned over and tapped over my heart. "From a humble and sincere place."

"Oh." *Was I humble?* Maybe. *Was I sincere?* I thought so. I hoped I was enough to have my prayers answered. But what did that even look like? A voice saying, "Alaina, you are humble and sincere. Now I will answer your prayers. Eat a bunch of peanuts, because you know what they do to you. Turn your bottom toward the shadow monster and let it rip. Farts that will choke it to death." *Really Alaina? At a time like this? See, that's why people don't believe you are thirteen.*

My grandmother started to stand as if there was nothing more to be said.

"Uh, Grandma? I was wondering…Why do you need such a big house for only you?"

"She looked down at me. "Because I live in a world where others need a place to stay. Where they will be safe—hidden until an appointed time. We all have a role to play on this journey. I have many."

My expression must have said, *"What in the world?"* because she laughed.

"Alaina, it's Mom," Leif yelled.

"It is? On the phone?"

"No. On the shoe."

I ran to the phone and snatched it from Leif. The first thing I wanted to ask my mother was about this gleamer stuff and how come she hadn't told me about it. But Grandma Eleanor shook her head as if she knew what I was thinking.

"Mom, hi! I miss you."

"I miss you too, and so does your father. I have some news. What do you want to hear first, the good or the bad?"

"The bad, I guess."

"Your father isn't feeling well. But the good news is we're coming back early, so you can come home—"

"Really?" I thought of leaving my new friends and what would happen if I left. Everyone in Muskegon, including my grandmother and Sheena Meyer would be doomed. And my fate was attached to hers in some way. "No."

"No?"

"I mean, we shouldn't take our time away from Grandma. She hasn't seen us in so long and she always gets two weeks with us. In fact, we should stay until January second. That way dad can get better and relax without us there."

"Wow. I certainly didn't expect this reaction. Are you sure? I guess I could check and see about changing your flights. So you're saying that you are not ready to come home?"

"Not yet. Don't punish us and Grandma because dad got sick." *That's right, throw a guilt trip on her.*

"Well—"

"Okay, thanks, Mom. Tell Daddy that I hope he gets better quickly. Gotta go. Love you. Kiss kiss." I hung up the phone.

That night, on my way to bed, I stood in the hall listening to Mintz and my grandmother.

"They shouldn't go back to the youth center."

"They want to."

"But something could happen, and I may not be there next time to help them. Thank goodness the hope of those kids with them was off the charts."

"You're awfully grumpy this evening, Mintz."

"When has that changed? So are you going to tell her?"

Mintz mumbled something more, and I wished I had gotten a glass and placed it against the wall with my ear to it, so I could hear better.

"Tell her *what*?" asked Grandma Eleanor. "She knows that her gifts are a blessing, meant to be used to spread light and hope in a world threatened by darkness."

"So you didn't tell her that she's a chrono gleamer then?"

"I don't have to. You just did. Come in, Alaina."

Chapter Fourteen

I froze in the hallway, my eyes wide, startled that my grandmother had known I was listening. Slowly, I pushed open the door to the sitting room and stepped inside. Mintz hovered behind a chair, looking smug.

I shifted my weight from one foot to the other, my shoes scraping softly against the floor as I nervously shuffled my feet, unable to stand still. I felt guilty for eavesdropping, but I was also burning with curiosity. "I'm sorry," I said softly.

"No, you're not." Grandma Eleanor patted the ottoman beside her chair, and I sat.

"I'll see you tomorrow," said Mintz. "Have a good night, ladies."

My grandmother gave me a knowing glance. "Ask me one question. Just one, and then head up to bed. The question that is burning inside you."

I had so many. How could I choose just one? "What is a chrono gleamer and why am I one?"

"That's two questions. I will answer the first. A chrono gleamer is a type of traveler gleamer, meaning you can gleam through time itself like pages in a book you can turn to and read as you wish."

My eyes were wide as I tried to grasp what she was telling me. *Gleam through time? That's what Chana was trying to explain to me.*

"The Murk can't find out what you are. Travelers see what it can't and therefore can thwart its plans."

I took a deep breath, grabbed my grandmother's mug (the size of a soup bowl) and almost burned my tongue, mouth, and esophagus, gulping down the bitter tea.

She chuckled. "Did that help?"

I nodded and wiped my mouth on the back of my hand. "So I can see the future?"

"Not quite," Grandmother Eleanor said. "Think of it more like...glimpses. The future is always in motion, ever changing. Your gift allows you to gleam possibilities, insights—but nothing in the future is ever certain."

I frowned. The whole thing sounded complicated. And a little scary.

"It is the only reason you are able to see what you've seen via the Aetates Papilio," she calmly continued. "For some, it is a book of stories about gleamers, but for most it is just a book of blank pages. For you, it changes as it needs to—to help."

"So . . . the Aetates Papilio chooses what I see?" I asked, trying to understand.

"In a way," my grandmother replied. "Your gift works in conjunction with the Aetates Papilio to show you what is most important for you to see at that time."

"So, it's a magical book."

"I've told you before, there is no such thing as magic."

"Then how does it work?"

"You wouldn't believe me if I told you."

"Please, Grandma. That's the last question I will ask tonight."

"Angels."

"Angels," I repeated.

Grandmother Eleanor nodded. "Helpers from Him," she said with a quick lift of her head toward the ceiling. "The Aetates Papilio was crafted long ago with divine guidance and reveals that which needs to be conveyed to a gleamer."

"A chrono gleamer."

"Yes.'"

Before I could ask any more questions (even though I said I wouldn't), a loud clatter from the kitchen made us both jump. I glanced nervously at Grandma Eleanor.

"Stay here," she said, rising from her chair. "I'll go and check it out."

She left the room, and I looked out into the hall after her. She didn't grab a bat, hockey stick, or one of her heavy vases to hit the intruder with. I feared for her life, and looked around for something I could charge in and knock someone over the head with.

Muted voices came from the kitchen. Grandma Eleanor was speaking to someone. Calmly. Curiosity propelled me out of the sitting room towards the kitchen.

I crept down the hallway as quietly as I could, not wanting Grandma Eleanor to know I had disobeyed her. As I got closer to the kitchen, I could make out two voices. One belonged to my grandmother. The other was unfamiliar—a woman she called Valerie.

"My grandchildren are here," my grandmother was saying. "Why can't they go to your house?"

"Because everyone is safe at Shiloh. That's why you built this monstrous home." Her voice sounded older, like my father's mother, Grandma Ruth.

"I should never have given you a key."

"Who else is going to check in on you? Mintz? Would it kill her to have a genuine smile once in a while?"

"Sorry, I broke your dish," said a kid's voice.

"How long?"

"I don't know. It's been seen at his school. And he thinks he saw it today. I told his mother he would be safe. Though I doubt she understood anything I said, in the state she was in."

"She drinks," said the boy.

"Glory be, I'm going to need you to stop giving up information so easily."

"Then it knows he's a gleamer?" asked Grandma Eleanor.

"Yes."

"Then—"

Before I could hear more, a hand grabbed my shoulder. I whirled around to see my brother looking at me over the rail of the stairs with curious eyes. He put a finger to his lips, then pointed down the hall, and I followed him away from the kitchen.

"Why are you up?" I asked once we were inside the sitting room.

"I heard noises and got curious." He giggled. "I caught you snooping. Grandma's got company? What's going on?"

"I don't know exactly," I whispered back. "Did you hear what they were saying?"

Leif shook his head.

Before I could ask him anything else, we heard footsteps approaching from the kitchen. Leif and I scurried and plopped down on chairs, trying our best to look casual.

A moment later, Grandma Eleanor appeared in the doorway. "Everything's fine—oh, Leif, did we wake you? An old friend stopped by." She smiled, but it seemed forced. Who was this Valerie person? She seemed to know my grandmother pretty well—well enough to have a key to the house. But she had never mentioned her before.

Grandma Eleanor sent us up to bed and never mentioned the kid or that someone else would be sleeping in the same house with us. I could wake with the person all creepy, standing over my bed. So as soon as the house was quiet, I went down to Leif's room, locked the door behind me, and climbed in bed with him.

I woke at 3 a.m. and told myself to go back to sleep. Minutes later, I tiptoed back to the library expecting to find it locked, but the door opened. I hesitated for a second, then walked over and brushed my fingers over the cover of the book. Warmth spread through my hand and a golden light radiated from its pages.

As I opened the book, words formed a story within the golden light. It began with a young girl, just thirteen years old, who discovered she was a gleamer and sought the wisdom of the gleaming book to find a way to stop the dark forces threatening her world. Then the book's narrative spoke directly to me: Only a chrono gleamer, chosen by the Almighty, can unlock the secrets woven through time.

"I know all of that. Well, except for the chosen part. But can I really do this?"

I read further and a verse stood out among the rest, its words glowing: "For I know the plans I have for you, declares the Lord, plans to prosper you and not to harm you, plans to give you hope and a future," I read in a whisper. This was different from anything I had read thus far. I stopped reading, overwhelmed and realizing I needed to figure out what to do or where to go from here. I closed my eyes and prayed.

When I picked up the book again, there was a bold typed message: **Complete your mission by Christmas, and light will triumph over darkness.**

Christmas? That was only a week away. I thought I had until New Year's Day. That's what Chana had said.

Then I remembered Grandma Eleanor mentioning the future was constantly in motion, so something must have changed. I thought for a moment. *Something happened that made things more urgent. I can't do this. An adult needs to do this.* For a moment, I wondered if Sheena Meyer felt the same. If she knew she was a gleamer and if she did, how she handled it.

I went back to the book and read on: *She wants to stop what is happening to her. She doesn't want this.*

"What? I didn't say that."

She is in denial. She wants to go back to the way things used to be and not be a gleamer.

"That's a lie."

She wants to go home to Penelope and Noah and life in North Carolina.

"I didn't say that!"

Alaina must face the truth . . . She does not want to be a gleamer.

Chapter Fifteen

Dust particles danced in the beams of light coming from the table lamp. I stood with clenched fists looking down at the book. "Okay, you're right. Why would I want to be a gleamer!" I screamed, slamming the book shut, tempted to throw it across the room. "I'm only thirteen," I said with tears in my eyes. "I didn't ask for this."

I sat on the floor with my head in my hands, overwhelmed. I was just an ordinary girl—at least I thought I was—unaware of this whole other world taking place in the shadows of my world.

After a few minutes passed, I composed myself and slowly stood, my cheeks wet with tears. I stared at the book I had just slammed shut. The cover no longer glowed, the words now hidden from view. "I . . . I didn't mean that," I whispered, wiping at my eyes with the sleeve of my pajama top. "I'm sorry, God. I'm just . . . I'm scared." It was probably the most honest I had ever been.

I took a deep, shaky breath and cautiously reopened the book. The pages had returned to the beginning, as if the whole incident had never happened.

"I'm sorry," I repeated. "I know you have a plan for me. I just . . . I'm not sure I'm ready for this."

A gentle breeze ruffled the pages. The book emitted a faint glow. When the pages finally stopped turning, they revealed a letter—addressed to me.

Dearest Alaina,

I understand your plight, but know this: I see the bravery and compassion within your heart, qualities that far outweigh your age. I see the hope and faith you are unaware you have.

Remember the verse you read. May it strengthen you in the hardest of times: For I know the plans I have for you . . . Seek His guidance, and you will find the strength and wisdom you need.

In due time, you will understand.

"Wait, who is this from?"

As if in response, a soft glow filled the room. My breath caught in my chest as a towering figure appeared before me, every inch of it glowing with energy.

My breath caught in my chest as I tried to make sense of what I was seeing. *What is happening? Should I run? No, don't run. Yeah, Run!*

"Do not be afraid," the angel spoke softly in my mind.

"O-okay . . . h-hey . . . th-there."

It extended a shimmering hand.

"W-what? As in touch?" I stammered, unsure of what to do.

The angel waited, patient and calm. I hesitated. *What is happening*, I whined again inside. Yet, despite the uncertainty, I felt a strange sense of trust. Slowly, I reached my hand forward, trembling as our hands met.

The moment our fingers touched, a rush of warmth enveloped me, and the room around us began to blur and fade. The walls dissolved into a cascade of light, and I felt myself being gently lifted, as though the air carried me.

When the light cleared, we were no longer in the library. Instead, we stood in the heart of downtown, near the Muskegon Together Rising sculpture in the traffic circle. Snow blanketed the streets, sparkling under the soft glow of Christmas lights that adorned every lamppost and that connected to the sculpture. Every tree and storefront was also decorated in lights. The air was crisp, against my skin, filled with the mingling scents of pine, cinnamon, and donuts and apple cider.

But it wasn't just the decorations and scents that stood out to me—it was the people. Their faces radiated joy and peace. They greeted each other with warm hugs, their laughter filling the air like music. Down the road, families gathered around the Christmas tree at Hackley Park, sharing smiles and love.

"This is the future that awaits," the angel's voice echoed inside me. "After the darkness is defeated."

"Now, you must see the opposite of this reality," the angel's tone didn't change but the words gave me chills.

The scene shifted, and I found myself still in Muskegon, but it was nothing like before. The streets were empty, the snow turned to slush, dirty and in mounds against the curbs. The Christmas lights flickered weakly, some out altogether. The festive decorations were torn down.

Shadows loomed over the city. The people were there, but this time they were different. Their faces were no longer bright. They walked through the streets alone, shoulders hunched, eyes hollow. And there was an eerie silence, broken only by the occasional echo of a distant, mournful cry.

The joy that had radiated from the city was gone, replaced by a sense of hopelessness.

"The darkness you see has taken root in their hearts," the angel said. "When the light is lost, so too is the spirit of the people. This is the world where the Murk prevails, where fear and despair reign."

I watched in horror as families drifted apart, their bonds broken, their faces twisted in pain and anger. They no longer looked at one another with love but with suspicion and distrust. And one of them I recognized . . . Sir Ballard.

"They are lost to darkness," the angel continued. "Without the light of hope, they cannot find their way back. The Murk feeds on their despair and fears, turning them against each other, against themselves. This is what could be, if you do not succeed."

Tears welled in my eyes as I took in the bleak scene.

"Remember this, Child." The angel's voice pulled me from my thoughts, its tone urgent but gentle. As the vision of the darkened Muskegon began to fade and I was again surrounded by the books of my grandmother's library, the angel's next words echoed in my mind. "May your vision be true."

"I'll do my best," I replied, my voice raspy with emotion.

And just like that, the angel disappeared, leaving its lingering peace.

I left the library and closed the door behind me. My mind was no longer filled with worry. My steps were determined as I climbed the stairs. I checked on Leif and then went to my own bedroom, no longer worried about anyone sneaking in on me.

A few hours later I slowly opened my eyes and screamed, seeing someone standing over me.

"Why is your first reaction to scream? Punch instead."

"What?"

"You've slept in so late. Are you going today or not?"

"Ms. Mintz? Why are you in my room?"

"Because I've been calling you for a half hour."

"Have you?"

I sat up, trying to think clearly. "Oh, to the center. Yes, I'm going. Is Leif up?"

"He's waiting in the kitchen. Hurry up, sleepyhead."

Was Mintz being nice? I could hardly tell. She had one tone and one expression, usually.

As I washed my face, I stared at myself in the mirror. Everything that happened the day before seemed only a dream now. I picked up my phone and dialed.

"Penelope!"

"Alaina! It's about time. What took you so long to call? Noah came skating with us."

"I don't care about Noah anymore."

"You don't care about Noah? Is this Alaina I'm speaking with? Alaina Marie Thompson?"

"The one and only."

"Oh my gosh! You met someone else, didn't you? Tell me all about him and don't leave anything out. Then, I'll tell Noah and make him jealous."

"Don't do that, Pen. I'm calling because I need your help with something."

"Concerning that book?"

"Kind of."

"Did using the chatbot help?"

"It actually did. But how can I help save a girl who doesn't even know that I exist?"

"Ummm . . . Mom, I'm on the phone. Yes, with Alaina. She's fine," she yelled. "Become her."

"Excuse me?"

"I don't know where that just came from. It just popped into my head. Maybe I saw it in a movie. Anyway, to understand her and what she is going through, become her. Meaning, put yourself in her shoes. Then, you will know all about her and what she specifically needs."

"Become her . . . " I thought aloud. "Pen, I think you just came through for me."

"Don't I always?"

"Alaina!" Mintz called.

"Oops, gotta go."

"Okay. Call me back. For real this time."

"Will do."

When I made it downstairs, Grandma Eleanor wasn't there. "She's gone out for the day," said Mintz.

"With last night's visitor?" I asked.

"Here," she said, holding out sack lunches to me and Leif. "Grab your boots, coats, sneakers, or whatever you wear. Let's go."

I wasn't the slightest bit surprised that Mintz ignored my question. She drove us to the center and for some reason chose to turn down Strong Avenue and drove right past Sheena Meyer's house. That brought the reality of everything back to me.

When we arrived at the youth center, Mintz signed us in, and we hurried off to the gymnasium. Alaysia ran to me as soon as she saw me.

"Alaina! I thought you might not come back. Don't you know how to answer your emails?"

Leif ran to his friends.

"I haven't checked them. I didn't get a chance to. But you know, normal people exchange phone numbers."

"Yeah, but I didn't know if you were worthy of my number yet," she joked.

Selah, Sahara, and Anthony ran over. "We're in," Selah declared confidently.

"What?" I asked, confused.

"We talked about it all night," Alaysia explained. "Whatever help you need, we're in." Her siblings nodded in agreement.

"No. This is too dangerous. Wait, how do you know I need help?"

Alaina pointed at the book under her arm. "I think we're the dwarfs in Stephen Woodruff's book."

I hadn't been in the mood to laugh in a while, but at that moment, I howled like I hadn't in months.

"This is not a funny matter," Alaysia said with a grin. "And what kind of friends would we be if we didn't help each other out?"

Leif came bounding over, his curly hair bouncing. "Alaina! They have foosball and air hockey here too! Can I go play?"

"Just stay where I can see you," I said following him into the adjoining room. Alaysia and her siblings came along. Watching Leif, I felt a little envious of his carefree spirit. If only I could enjoy being a kid again, instead of dealing with this gleamer stuff.

"All right, troops, let's huddle up," Selah said in an exaggerated coach-voice, waving everyone over."

"Oh you're in charge now?" asked Alaysia.

"I'm just getting the meeting started," Selah replied.

"Okay, thanks for that," I told her. "I have an idea. You guys were here last year. How hard is it to sneak out of the center for a bit?"

"A prison break? This should be interesting," said Alaysia.

"It's not hard if you leave by the basement window."

We all turned to see who said that.

"Deuce, why are you always coming out of nowhere? Don't you know it's not polite to sneak up on people?" asked Sahara.

He pushed his glasses up on his nose. "I didn't sneak up on you. And since you're having this conversation in front of everybody, I thought it was open to the public."

"He's right, though," I replied. "But someone will have to stay here as a lookout."

"Sahara," her siblings replied.

"No, not me."

"You're always hurting yourself," said Alaysia.

"No, it has to be Anthony. Leif and all the other boys will be looking for him."

"True," said Alaysia. "We'll go. You stay, Anthony."

"When are we doing it?"

"After lunch," I replied.

"But there are less kids here then," said Sahara.

"That's why they won't look for us. They will think we left without signing out. Then, when we come back and they see us, they will say, 'Oh, I didn't know you were still here," said Alaysia.

"It's a good plan. But I need enthusiastic, hardworking, and positive people on my team. Can you level-up to join the A-Team?" I asked, joking.

Alaysia grinned.

"We're in," they each replied.

"Good because I would've offered you money next."

"And we would have taken it," said Sahara.

I felt good about the plan and relieved I wouldn't have to do it alone. But why were my legs shaking?

After we left the gym, it was craft time, and we made wreaths. Next, we played kickball and then participated in the hip hop dance class. When I entered the cafeteria for lunch, I noticed Sir Ballard glaring at me.

I walked right over to him. "You seem to have a problem with me. Or is it with everyone?"

Sir frowned. "I don't get you and this place."

"The youth center?"

"Yeah, why are you here?"

"I come here every year."

"Because . . ."

"Why are you asking?"

"I see the SUV's you arrive in. You brought your own lunch today. Look around, everyone isn't like you."

"Why would they need to be?"

"Some of us are here 'cause our parents are working or running errands. Either we're too young to stay home alone, or we're older, and they don't trust us. Others have nothing better to do, so their parents are basically forcing them to stay busy over winter break. I mean, that's what they get the funding for, for this place," he said looking around the room. "For me, it's so I can make sure me and my brother have something to eat now that school is out. You don't know what that's like, do you? Having to go where they feed you breakfast and lunch, like during the school year, so you get a decent meal?"

"I don't. I'm really sorry you have to deal with that." I said, not knowing what else to say or why he even overshared in the first place.

"Hmph, some gleamer," Sir said and walked away.

Chapter Sixteen

y mouth dropped. *Did he just—*

My heart pounded so hard that I could hear it and it drowned out every other sound in the cafeteria. "What did you just say?" I demanded.

Sir turned back and lowered his voice. "I said, some gleamer you are. You don't even know what you're doing, do you?"

How could he possibly know about gleamers? How did he know I was one? I tried to stay calm. "I have no idea what you're talking about," I replied and tried to laugh like it was the most absurd, funny thing.

"Yeah, okay," he replied.

Sir walked away, leaving me sitting there in shock. Patrick, and the rest of the crew that seemed to migrate together each day, sat around me as if they were playing musical chairs and might lose a seat. I glanced over at Sir. He seemed angry and distrustful, and almost jealous of the fact that I wasn't poor. I wasn't rich either. My grandmother might be, but I sure wasn't. But that did not explain how he knew my secret.

Opening my sack lunch gave my shaking hands something to do, and I reminded myself that there were more pressing matters to deal with right now—like getting up the nerve to leave the center without permission. A Red Delicious apple sat on top of the bag, so I grabbed it and bit down, chewing fast before taking another bite. My stomach immediately twisted from anxiety. I shook my head telling myself: *Don't get overwhelmed. One mystery at a time, Alaina. Handle one mystery at a time.*

After lunch, the staff was in that zone where they were full and a little tired. My mom called it a post-lunch dip. Instructors were talking, rather than focusing on us, and probably figuring we were good wholesome kids being where we were supposed to be and doing what we were supposed to do.

"I eat so much over the holidays. My doctor is going to kill me. My yearly physical is always right after the holidays. I can hear him now, elevated cholesterol blah blah blah," one of them said.

"Well, this time of year is the best time to put on weight for a role."

"You're not an actress."

"Oh!" They fell into each other laughing.

"See, they're not even paying attention to anything right now," I whispered. "Let's go."

Alaysia pointed ahead of us at the wall of coats.

"Oh, yeah. We need those."

We backed up around the corner. "This is what we'll do," said Anthony. "We can stash your coats close by the basement door—like in a utility closet or under a bench or something. Then you can grab them on the way out."

"Or we can all say we're cold and keep our coats on," said Sahara.

"Seems easier," I replied.

Anthony shook his head. "I don't agree, but whatever."

"But how do we even get to the basement?" asked Selah.

I thought for a moment. "Books."

"Books?"

A half hour later, we went to the library. "Put your hands out Anthony."

He extended his arms, and I placed books on top of them. The girls realized what I was doing and grabbed more books.

"This is getting heavy," said Anthony.

"That's the point."

"That's enough," he said after we could no longer see his face over the stack.

"Now walk this way," I said and guided him.

"Slow down. I can't see. I'm going to drop them."

Once we got him further away from the basement door, I told him, "Count to ten and then drop them."

We shot down the hall and hid around the corner. When we heard the books drop and Anthony scream (he added that on his own) and the youth center staff came rushing to investigate, we hurried down the narrow stairs to the basement utility room. The air was musty, exposed wiring hung from the ceiling, and the walls were lined with shelves cluttered with forgotten supplies—paint cans, old tools, and bins.

"Are you ready for this?" Alaysia asked under her breath.

Don't tell her you're terrified. "As ready as I'm going to get," I said, though my heart pounded like a drum.

"Good. But I don't see a ladder," she replied, looking around us.

"But there are crates down here," Sahara pointed out, already moving quickly. She stacked the old wooden crates near a small, grimy window, each one wobbling slightly as she built our makeshift escape route. The window, half-covered in cobwebs, was barely large enough to squeeze through, but we did, careful to close it quietly.

Alaysia crouched down and used her gloved hand to swipe over the fresh snow. "There," she said, triumphantly pointing at the snow. "No tracks, means no kids left this way."

"But we are making more tracks as we walk," said Sahara.

"Well help me brush them away while we back up."

"We'll have to do that all the way to the street!"

I couldn't believe they were having a whole discussion about this. "You guys are going to get us caught. Let's just go."

Alaysia gave the ground one last swipe before following us. Oddly, it felt like we'd been locked away in prison and were now free to inhale the fresh air and live our lives.

"Which way, Alaina?" asked Alaysia.

"Around the side of the building," I replied and hurried that way, hunched down, though there were no windows on that end.

"Slow down, A-Team, or whatever you call yourselves," said Sahara.

"Look, you wanted to come, so keep up," said Alaysia.

We ran up Southern Ave and turned up Sixth Street. "Is this the right way?" asked Selah.

"Yes!" at least I thought it was. Then I saw the sign for Strong Avenue. "It's right down here."

We walked down the street looking around at each house and the cars that passed like someone might say, "I see you. You escaped from the youth center." Then it dawned on me... "You guys never asked why I wanted to leave or what we were going to do out here."

"You're looking for *her*..." said Alaysia.

I was confused. "Her who?"

"The princess—"

"Are you back to that book again?" asked Sahara.

"Yes, I'm telling you it correlates with what's happening."

"When did you start using words like correlates?" asked Selah.

"Stay focused. Alaina, what I know is that you need something from her."

"What do I need?" I really wanted to know because I had no idea what I was going to do once I got to Sheena Meyer's house.

"You'll know when you get there," said Alaysia.

"I hope so," I said, stopping in front of the house.

"This is it?" she asked.

I slowly nodded, suddenly wanting to turn around and go back the way we came.

"Sahara, no!"

She ran up the porch steps and rang the doorbell.

"Why did you do that?"

"Because you're wasting time and we have to get back before they notice we're gone." She opened the screened door and walked onto the porch.

"Get your sister. She's doing too much," I told Alaysia.

We hurried behind her as a woman wearing one of those turbans that dried your hair opened the front door. "Hello."

I didn't know if we were stunned or if they were waiting for me to say something, but we all stood there staring at her.

"Are you okay?"

"On . . . " I cleared my throat. "On the first day of Christmas . . . " I started singing and the girls joined in. "A partridge in a pear tree . . . "

She grinned. "You're carolers?" She held a hand up stopping us. "You didn't do this correctly. You're supposed to sing from outside."

"We were cold."

"Hold on a minute. I've got something for you." She disappeared inside the house leaving the door cracked open. I carefully pushed it back, seeing the foyer and living room off to the right, and stairs to the left.

Then I noticed one of the coats hanging from hooks by the door. *That's it! That's the coat Sheena was wearing when she helped push Grandma Eleanor's car out of her driveway.* I snatched it from the hook and passed it behind me to Alaysia, who placed it under her coat, making her appear to have gained thirty pounds.

The woman came back with four beige cups resembling the ones from Starbucks and handed them to us.

"What's this?" I asked.

"Mushroom hot chocolate. It's much healthier. It will keep you warm. You'll like it. You'll see."

"Thank you," we said.

"I'm glad you're caroling during the day instead of at night since there are no adults with you, but stay on the sidewalk okay. Wait a minute." She left again and came back with a whistle. "Blow this if anything seems off." She looked up and down the street. I can't vouch for everyone on this street."

"Okay, thanks. See you," said Alaysia.

"Is Sheena here?" I got up the nerve to ask.

"You know my daughter? No she's not. What's your name? I'll tell her you stopped by."

"Uh, Chana?" *Sheesh. Why couldn't I think of another name? I could have even said, Penelope.*

She looked confused. "She knows two Chana's? Okay. Be blessed girls." She waved and closed the door.

We walked away. "Keep going," I said. "She may be watching from the window."

Sahara sipped the hot chocolate and spit it out on the sidewalk coughing. The splotchy brown stains seeped into the snow. "It's disgusting. She's trying to kill us."

Selah took a sip. "There's no sugar in it."

"At least it's hot," said Alaina, holding her stomach with one hand to make sure the coat didn't fall out. "So why did we just steal someone's coat?"

"There's no way we're getting into heaven after this," said Selah.

"Yes we are. We're only borrowing it. Plus we're helping Alaina. This is for a good cause, right, Alaina?"

"Absolutely."

"And by Sheena, did you mean Sheena Meyer?"

I stopped walking. "You know her?"

"Yeah, she used to come to the center sometimes with Chana. Not so much during winter break, but during summer break when we're in town, she comes."

"What do you know about her?"

"Nothing really. She's nice. Different."

"Different how? She can't dance and she doesn't really listen to the music everyone else listens to, and she doesn't care about fashion or social media."

"Then what does she care about?"

"Saving the earth."

My eyes grew wide.

"You know, recycling and stuff."

"Oh."

"Hey, I think those boys are watching us," Selah said.

They were across the street, headed to a car in front of some townhomes, laughing and goofing around. Suddenly, someone from their group spotted us and they all turned toward us. "Aren't you cold? Don't you want to come over and hang out with us?" one of them called out. "We can all go inside and get warm. We'll order pizza."

We kept walking, acting like we didn't hear them.

"Come on," another one said. "We won't bite."

I picked up my pace, keeping my eyes fixed ahead. Couldn't they see how young some of us were?

"Just ignore them," Alaysia said under her breath. Sahara and Selah were on either side of her, staying close.

The streets were mostly empty, with only a few passing cars splashing slush over the park strip.

The boys persisted, trailing behind at a distance as they continued to call out. "What's the rush? We're just being friendly! Slowdown!"

"Do not slow down," I said and started jogging.

As we turned a corner, the sidewalk narrowed, flanked by towering snowbanks crusted with ice from the snowplow trucks. My pulse quickened. We turned up the wrong street. If the boys tried to confront us here, we would be trapped. Why couldn't they just leave us alone?

On the other side of the snowbanks were the sprawling brick walls of the youth center. "You guys go." I told them. "I'll—I don't know what I will do, but it will give you a chance to climb over.

"We're not leaving you," said Selah.

"And I'm not letting you stay," said Alaysia.

I glanced back at the boys who were getting closer. "We're right behind the building. Just go. I'll lead them away."

"You sure don't know how to follow orders. I told you to slow down," said the boy closest to us.

My friends refused to leave, and I hoped that being a gleamer would somehow protect us or make the boys move on.

I stood in front of my friends. "Leave us alone," I said, holding up the whistle. Something needed to happen before I had to put my mouth on someone's random whistle.

"Scared now, aren't ya? Make me," said the boy. He was the only one talking. The others only smirked.

"You're going to get lumps of coal for Christmas!" yelled Sahara.

Even I looked at her like, *What in the world?*

"Don't tell me you believe in that stuff," the boy yelled back.

"Do you?" I asked her.

"Nope. I just hoped they did," said Sahara.

"I don't know why. Clearly, they don't care about doing the right thing or going to heaven one day as much as we do," said Selah. She looked up at the sky. "Whoever is controlling this video game, please increase our strength–and give us good weapons!"

"This is no time to joke around," said Alaysia.

Suddenly, Selah and Sahara pushed me behind them and Alaysia positioned herself in front of her sisters. They all held fighting stances.

"You guys know karate?" I asked.

"No, but in our family, if one fights, we all fight. You're family now, Alaina," said Alaysia. "Don't worry. If I get punched in the stomach, I won't feel anything through this extra coat."

The boys were getting closer.

"Do you hear that beeping—like an alarm?" asked Selah.

"A little, but my heart is pounding so hard I can barely hear *you*." Then I got the craziest idea. "Hey, we're gonna run at them screaming, like something is after us."

"Do you think that will work?" asked Alaysia.

"We don't have any other options."

They didn't give me a chance to count off and all started screaming and running, and I made sure I had the most frightened expression I could muster.

The boys started backing up. The biggest one looked around frantically and shouted, "We need to get the heck out of here, now!" They all bolted at once, their feet pounding against the road, some slipping on ice and getting back up and running.

We quieted and stopped. "See? Told you." Relief washed over my friend's faces.

Though our screaming had stopped, we could still hear screaming. We looked behind us. Kids were charging toward us from the youth center, a kaleidoscope of coats flying behind them.

I couldn't believe my eyes. "It wasn't us, it was them..."

Anthony made it to us first. Leif was right behind him along with Alaysia's youngest sister, Zariyah. "Are you guys okay?"

"What are you doing out here?"

"Sir told us you needed help, so I pulled the fire alarm. Everyone is outside so they won't notice you coming back in with everyone."

"But you're all running this way screaming."

"Sir told us to."

"He did?" *How did he know?*

Chapter Seventeen

"You won the race!" the kids told Anthony as they approached.

"No, he didn't," said a boy. He pointed at us. "They were so fast that they climbed over the fence. Showoffs!"

"Yep. Sure did!" said Sahara. "Broken leg and all."

"Stop it. Your leg is not broken," said Alaysia.

I glanced around, half expecting to see a host of angels, or maybe just one, hovering nearby, but there was no sign of any.

The rest of the screaming kids from the youth center stopped running when they got to the fence. Here they were, providing the perfect distraction so we could slip back inside unnoticed.

Fire truck sirens rang out as they pulled up in front of the center. It didn't take long before we were given the all clear to go back inside.

I grabbed Leif's hand tightly as we joined the crowd of kids flooding back into the youth center. Once inside, while the other kids were still milling around, chattering excitedly about the fire alarm, we hurried to the quiet room. I collapsed onto one of the beanbag chairs.

"That was close," said Alaysia, sinking down beside me and tossing Sheena's coat onto my head.

I snatched it off and studied it. "Too close. How did Sir know? And where is he?"

"I don't know. He's mysterious like that," said Anthony. "I think he might be psychic or something."

I smiled faintly, suspecting there was more to Sir than any of them realized.

"We should split up. Come on, Leif," said Anthony. "We have tag today."

"Yay!" said Leif.

"I'm going to go and hug a furnace," said Sahara.

I put on the coat. It was just a little big on me. I was small for my age, and I knew it—the reason people thought I was younger than thirteen. I reached into the pockets and pulled out a slip of paper. Written on it was: *Mr. Tobias*. And there was a phone number.

Wait, didn't Grandma Eleanor use that name before? I closed my eyes, trying to remember. The memory came into sharp focus as if I were standing there again. It couldn't have been more than five years ago. I could almost feel the stuffiness of the hallway back then and the cool floorboards under my bare feet. I pictured me stopping under each picture in the hall.

"Grammy, that man keeps looking at me."

"Who, sweetie?"

I pulled her to the photo.

"Him?"

"Uh-huh."

"That's Tobias. He's harmless honey—family. You met him a long time ago. Unfortunately you'll never get to visit with him." She stared off into the distance for a moment. "Or will you . . ."

I opened my eyes. I did it. I relived it all as if I were really there. I smiled to myself. *I've got the chrono gleamer thing down!*

If Sheena had his number, I needed to know why. After all, like Penelope said, I needed to become her.

Ducking into an empty office, I took out my cell phone and quickly dialed, not knowing what I was going to say. But winging it had always been my M.O.

After three rings, someone answered. "Hello?" came a man's groggy voice.

"Hi, is this Mr. Tobias?" I asked.

"Who wants to know?" the surly voice replied.

I swallowed. "My name is Alaina. Alaina Thompson. I . . . I think you know my grandmother, Eleanor?"

There was silence on the other end. Then, a heavy breath. "Eleanor's granddaughter, eh? I haven't seen you since you were knee high to a duck. Been wondering if you'd turn up one of these days. I know what you're after, but we shouldn't talk over the phone. Meet me at my home. Come alone, you hear?"

"But I don't have the address."

"You don't need it. That's how I will find out if you are truly Eleanor's granddaughter."

The call disconnected.

You've got to be kidding me.

I paced in front of the desk. On the one hand, I wanted backup in case anything went wrong. But on the other hand, Mr. Tobias had specifically told me to come alone. I didn't know him, so why should I trust him? But evidently Grandma Eleanor did. I mean, she had a giant picture of him on the wall along with the other . . . family. *Was he?*

I left the office and looked for Sir. I still needed to find out what he knew about gleamers and how he knew we needed help. But I heard someone laughing loudly.

"Grandma Eleanor?"

"Where have you been, Alaina? I sent Leif looking for you."

It occurred to me that she was here to pick us up early and if we hadn't gotten back when we did, she may have discovered that I had left the center.

"I was back there," I said, pointing behind me.

"Well get your things. Let's go."

I ran back peering in classrooms. "Psst, Alaysia . . . "

She turned, seeing me and ran over to the door.

"My grandmother is here to get us. I'll email you my number so I can text you like normal people, okay?"

"Yes, because I have so many questions."

"Okay, bye."

Leif ran up to me. "Grandma Eleanor sent me to find you."

I pushed him in front of me. "You weren't even looking. I saw you in there, playing. Get your coat."

"I found her," he yelled as we hurried to the front door.

"Sure you did. How was your day?" Grandma Eleanor asked as we headed out to her car.

"There is a tag competition tomorrow and they said I can join."

"What? Are you that good?"

"He really is," I replied.

"Then you're going to do it and I'll be there cheering you on. I don't care if you're just tying your shoes, I'll be the loudest one there."

Leif giggled.

"Uh . . . grandma . . . I need to make a stop."

"Where? For those red sugared Christmas caramel apples?"

"No. Mr. Tobias's house."

The car lurched to a sudden stop as Grandma Eleanor slammed on the brakes.

"Who's that?" asked Leif, but neither of us responded.

I glanced at her from the corner of my eye. Grandma Eleanor stared straight ahead. A second later, she started driving again.

We couldn't have driven for five minutes when she stopped again.

"Where are we?"

She pointed at a white house, with black shutters, on the right. "Mr. Tobias."

"Man, I'm starving," said Leif.

"He told me to come alone."

"No one is listening to me," said Leif.

"You've spoken to him?"

"On the phone for a second."

"You're both being disrespectful," said Leif.

"I see," Grandma Eleanor said with a nod. "Then we'll be waiting right here for you."

I hopped out of the car and walked up to the front door. I glanced back at the car and then knocked on the door. When no one answered, I rang the doorbell and held my breath as the door opened.

A woman wearing gray scrubs stood there. "Hello."

"Hi. Is Mr. Tobias here?"

"You're late!" he yelled from somewhere in the house.

"I guess he's expecting you. I'm Nurse Paige," she said while opening the door further and stepping back out of the way. "He's grumpy, but then again, when is he not? He's worse in the mornings," she whispered. "I'll leave you two alone."

Mr. Tobias rolled forward in a wheelchair. I recognized him immediately.

He was an old man, probably in his late eighties or early nineties, with wrinkled skin and thinning white hair. But his vibrant green eyes shone with intelligence and wisdom.

Furniture was positioned so he could get around easily with his wheelchair and there were angel figurines everywhere.

He squinted at me. "You don't understand your gift, do you?"

Was that the way he said hello? "No, I don't."

He shook his head. "Same as her."

"Who? Sheena Meyer?"

"Oh, you know about her, do you?"

"Very little."

"Hmph, I'll tell you this . . . Take everything you know and multiply it by one hundred and you will still know nothing." He looked deep into my eyes. "Oh my, you're a traveler." He wagged a finger. "One day, you'll join forces with another traveler, Aria. Remember that name. Speaking of names, do you know the meaning of yours?"

"No."

"Look it up."

All of this was well and good but why did he really ask me to come there? I didn't want to be rude. And I didn't want Grandma Eleanor waiting outside forever. "Mr. Tobias? What did you want to tell me?"

"Hmm . . . Oh, yes . . . Many years ago, darkness crept into the heart of a young man . . . Luke is his name. It twisted him, corrupted him, until he became obsessed with the one who could stop him."

"Sheena Meyer."

"Yes."

"There are many gleamers working together to keep her safe."

"Why her?"

"She has a very special gift, and she must live."

"And you are a gleamer?"

"Yes. A gleamer who knows things."

"Then . . . can you tell me how I am to help her? I've been told that—"

He finished the sentence for me. "That you are to save the city and the girl by Christmas and in saving her, you save yourself. That your fates are intertwined."

"Yes. So what do I do?"

"What you've been assigned. Enter the world beyond the veil and stop it."

"Stop what? You mean the Murk?"

"Let me put this in terms you will understand. The world is a computer program. The world has been infected by malware. Malware is the Murk. So you are..." he held his hand out toward me.

"Am I the anti-virus software?"

"You understand? Antivirus software is important, but it doesn't protect against all types of threats. Thus, you need different types of security programs. Thus, other types of gleamers."

"So what are you saying? I can kill it?"

He sat back in his chair. "No, no. Don't be silly. A traveler? No. That's Sheena Meyer's destiny. Yours is to put an end to what it's planning right now."

Lucky me, I said inside. But Mr. Tobias's piercing green eyes locked onto mine as if I had spoken the words directly to him. I shifted uncomfortably under his gaze. A flush of embarrassment rushed through my face, and I looked away.

"Indeed," he murmured. "See yourself out." He turned away, wheeling himself out of the room.

"Wait, that's it?"

"It is until it isn't," was his only reply.

Chapter Eighteen

I walked back outside and got into Grandma Eleanor's car.

"Well?" she asked eagerly.

"He told me more about Sheena Meyer and my fate," I said as we drove away from Mr. Tobias's house.

"And?"

"She has a special gift, and someone wants her dead."

"What else?"

"I have to stop it's plan," I answered quickly so that Leif wouldn't understand what I was talking about. But when I looked over my shoulder, he was fast asleep. "He also said to look up the meanings of our names and that our names weren't chosen randomly."

Grandma Eleanor started the car. "Your name, Alaina, has several meanings: precious, torch, rock. It also means light or bright. Leif, means heir."

I repeated the words to myself.

She glanced over at me. "You're like a precious gem. The light that shines within you, your torch, is vibrant."

"The gleam?"

"Yes."

"The rock part, that's your strength. You are stronger than you know."

I clicked in my seatbelt and sat back in my seat.

"Your name is who you are."

I grinned to myself.

She put the car in drive, and we rode up Monroe Street.

"Will you help me?" I asked.

"Honey, I wish I could. But I can do no more than heaven allows. We all have our own assignments and parts to play on this journey." We stopped at a light, and she lifted my chin. "However, that doesn't mean you're alone."

"You will be given everything you need to get through this. You will ask questions, you will cry, you will get discouraged . . . believe me, I know from experience. But every gleamer is given a measure of supernatural strength for what they are called to do."

"Grandma, will you be upset if I ask that we not talk for a while? I feel like my mind is on overload and about to explode."

She patted my hand. "Understood."

The rest of the car ride was silent as Grandma Eleanor drove us home. Leif slept soundly in the backseat, and I couldn't help but be envious of his peaceful rest. As if he nor anyone else had a worry in the world.

As we turned onto Grandma Eleanor's street, I thought of Sheena Meyer. She had to be a brave, extraordinary girl if she was destined to face the Murk itself. I shivered, despite the car's warmth. How could I possibly help someone with the ability to do that? What kind of gleamer was she?

The car rolled to a stop in front of the house. I stepped out into the crisp winter air, looking up at the second-floor windows under the eaves. Somewhere behind those windows, answers awaited.

One of those answers came running out of the front door. "He's gone!"

"Who?" I shouted as if Mintz was talking to me.

"And he took the book."

Mintz thought she lowered her voice enough that I wouldn't hear that part, but I did.

"What?" I exclaimed.

"If it falls into the wrong hands—"

"It's useless," said Grandma Eleanor.

"What about the stories it has already created? Do they remain after they've been read?" I asked.

Instead of answering, which I really needed her to do because my stories were in there, Grandma Eleanor turned to me. "Alaina, get your brother and go inside," she said sternly. Only this time, she checked to make sure we weren't listening to the rest of their conversation, so I heard nothing.

For the rest of the evening, Grandma Eleanor wasn't around. My parents called to check on us asking all kinds of questions about what we were doing for fun and I almost said, "Oh, fighting darkness and being a gleamer. Did you know about this?" But really, I didn't think they did. I mean, they didn't act like it at all. However, Grandma Eleanor was always odd, staring into my eyes over the years as if she were . . . waiting for it.

My eyes widened and I ran to the bathroom. That's how Sir knew. I brought my face close to the mirror and just before my nose touched it, I stared into my eyes. It took a minute, but a faint spark built within my pupils. The same spark I saw in Grandma Eleanor's eyes and Mr. Tobias's. The gleam.

I left the bathroom, went downstairs, and found Mintz in the kitchen. She poked around the refrigerator as I entered. "Don't worry about anything. Your grandmother's got it all under control."

"I think I should say the same to you," I replied as I neared her. I had never seen a hair of her bone straight bob out of place or eyeliner running before.

She wiped under her eyes. "You've got *me* tonight. What do you want for dinner?" Mintz asked, leaning against the kitchen counter.

"I can do spaghetti. It's the one dish I make very well."

"You?" She raised a perfectly arched eyebrow in surprise.

I grinned and took a step closer. "I've got skills."

Mintz turned to face me fully, and I took that chance to look deeply into her eyes. Finding what I was looking for, I nodded in satisfaction. "I'll need plenty of garlic."

"The pantry is all yours then," she said, gesturing towards the cabinet doors that opened to a room-sized pantry.

"Thanks," I replied, walked over and pulled at the cabinet doors that went all the way to the ceiling.

Inside, there sitting on the floor and holding the Aetates Papilio was . . . "Deuce?"

Chapter Nineteen

"Deuce?" I repeated, as if trying to convince myself that the annoying kid was really sitting on the pantry floor. But there he was.

Deuce looked up from the book with a start, his eyes wide behind his glasses. "Alaina! What are you doing here?" he exclaimed.

Mintz ran over, yanking me out of the way. She snatched the book from his hands.

"You know him?" she asked.

"He goes to the youth center."

I stared at him in confusion. "What am *I* doing here? What are *you* doing here?" I replied.

Wait, was this who I heard that Valerie person bringing in that night when the dish broke? Then I remembered that Grandma Eleanor said Shiloh was a place where she kept others safe.

Deuce and I exchanged bewildered glances. "This is my grandmother's house. They thought you ran away."

Deuce hesitated, then spoke softly. "I didn't run away. I haven't been at the center, because they've been . . . uh . . . protecting us."

"Protecting *us*? Who is *us*?"

"Me and my brother."

"Where is he?" asked Mintz.

"I don't know. Today, after you brought us back, he put me in here and I couldn't get out."

"I've told Eleanor about fixing this door. How did you get the book?"

"My brother shoved it into my hands when he put me in here."

"And this was okay with you?" I asked. "I mean, there's a window right there on the other end that you could have climbed out of."

"I don't know. I thought someone would find me sooner. Plus, this isn't such a bad place to be," he said, pushing his glasses up on his nose and looking around. "It's warm. There's food . . ."

Wrappers were all over the floor from where he'd had a feast.

"You need to clean this up," said Mintz.

Deuce hopped up and got to work picking up popcorn, and potato chip wrappers. "What's so special about this book?" he asked with his back to us.

The way he asked things always bothered me. And at that moment, I remembered Chana's warning about not trusting everyone. "It's a book of stories," I replied.

"You shouldn't have even been in the library in the first place. You should have stayed where you were," Mintz said and stormed away.

Deuce continued picking up the wrappers. "I didn't do it though. I told you my brother took the book and put me in here."

"Okay, well, I have to cook so . . ." If he was supposed to be in the house, what could I say? I moved around him and grabbed the items I needed for dinner and went about cooking. My spaghetti turned out perfectly and I showed Mintz how I used the leftovers to make spaghetti pie for the next day like my mother taught me. Not that it brought a smile to her face or that she was really even paying attention. She wouldn't eat. She mostly wrung her hands and paced, often biting on one fingernail and glancing over at us watching her. And she was a vault. Nothing I said could get her to share the slightest bit of information about what was happening in my grandmother's house or why she was always there, like she was a special agent or something.

When we turned in that night, Grandma Eleanor wasn't back yet. "Alaina," Mintz called as I led Leif up the stairs.

"Yes?"

"You cannot tell anyone he's here."

Duh, I'm not an idiot, I thought. "I figured," I replied.

The next day, it was as if none of it had ever happened. Grandma Eleanor made breakfast, our lunches were in bags on the counter, and Deuce was nowhere to be found. Leif and I actually searched all over the house looking for him.

Mintz dropped us off at the youth center because Grandma Eleanor didn't want us just waiting around the house while she "handled business." Whatever that meant.

"But what about the tag competition?" asked Leif.

"Don't worry. I'll be there," said Grandma Eleanor. "I wouldn't miss it for anything."

The youth center was bustling with activity when we arrived. As expected, Leif immediately spotted some of his friends and raced off to join them.

I wandered around a bit, trying to decide what I wanted to do first. Alaysia arrived and ran over, bombarding me with questions. "You didn't call or text last night. What happened? What did you do with Sheena's coat?"

"It's . . . a long story. But I'm going to get it back to her soon."

"How?"

"I don't know. She'll find it in her backyard or on her porch or something."

Alaysia narrowed her eyes. "This isn't some weird magical thing, is it?"

"There's no such thing as magic," I replied just like Grandma Eleanor would and walked away.

She followed me. "Well what is it then? We're a team, remember? Don't keep us in the dark. We put ourselves out there for you and whatever you're doing."

I stopped and talked fast. Anything to get her to stop talking about it. "There was a slip of paper in the pocket."

Her eyes widened.

"There was a name and phone number on it."

"You called it?"

"Yes, and he gave me an address to come to."

"And you went? Are you crazy?"

"My grandmother took me."

"Oh. So what happened. I mean, you don't look like you've been injured and you're here, so you didn't get taken and trapped in a basement or anything."

I shook my head. Usually I would have laughed because she was funny—a conspiracy-type person. "He told me things I needed to know."

Alaysia wagged a finger at me. "The mentor helping to prepare the hero for the quest. That's it. Just like in the—"

"Guess who just asked about you," interrupted Selah.

I spotted Patrick across the room and my heart did a little leap.

I played it off. "Who, Patrick? He just knows that if I'm here, Leif is here. They need him for the competition today."

"Oh, is that all it is?" Selah asked with a smirk.

I turned away so she wouldn't see me blush. If Patrick liked me—in a *you can have my last potato chip* or *I'll let you choose my character when we're down to the final boss while I'm gaming* kind of way—that would be one thing. But the truth was, I lived in North Carolina, and someone my age didn't have long-distance relationships. Not only that, he had no idea of who or what I really was and that was enough to scare the crush out of anyone.

"You looooove him," teased Alaysia's sister, Sahara in a singsong voice.

I rolled my eyes. "Nope. We're just friends—not even that really. You guys are my friends."

Leif ran over. "Alaina, come show me how to play four square!" He grabbed my hand, pulling me to the next room. I laughed and let him drag me along. The game was a good distraction, taking my mind off of everything for a while.

Chapter Twenty

As the day went on, I tried to subtly ask around about Deuce. But no one seemed to know much more than him being weird. Patrick said Deuce had only been coming to the youth center for about a month. He was pretty quiet most of the time unless he had questions about something. Where I was concerned, all he did was ask questions.

Alaysia mentioned that Deuce was really good at chess and usually played with some of the older kids. "He's autistic," a girl said, her words stumbling slightly as if she was searching for the right way to explain. "I've known him from school and remember it took a while for him to learn to talk. Or maybe he knew how but wasn't ready to be heard yet. I don't know how that whole thing works." She pointed at staff assistants walking in with bowls of popcorn. "Ooo . . . We're stringing popcorn for the tree? Is it fresh? I'm going to eat most of it," she said and hurried away.

"Watch, she's going to put butter on it," said Alaysia, "Someone go and tell Shay you don't put buttered popcorn on a tree."

After the next session, the director of the youth center announced over the loudspeaker that it was time for the weekly tag competition. This was one of the most popular events at the center. Kids eagerly started heading to the room where the huge tag arena was set up.

The teams gathered on opposite sides as the youth center volunteers explained the rules. I scanned the room for Grandma Eleanor and felt a pang of disappointment when she was nowhere to be seen, because I knew how badly Leif wanted her to be there.

Patrick grinned and shook Leif by the shoulders. "Are you ready? We're going to dominate!"

There were taggers and runners. Leif was a runner. The referee blew his whistle, and Leif shot away from the tagger.

Suddenly, a loud voice blared through a bullhorn, calling out his name. *I'm so embarrassed.* There was Grandma Eleanor, dressed like she was going to New York Fashion Week—heels, oversized sunglasses, fur-trimmed coat—and holding a bullhorn like it was her latest accessory. She waved it proudly, oblivious to the stares. I looked over at Leif, and the smile on his face as he ran, overshadowed my need to duck behind a wall.

The competition was intense. Kids leapt over obstacles, vaulted off walls, and swung from bars with agile precision. Sneakers squeaking and bodies thumping against padded barriers. One kid, the tagger, launched himself into the air, narrowly missing a leapfrog over a stack of mats as the runner, Sir, rolled away just in time.

It was a dizzying mix of speed and acrobatics. Shouts of encouragement and occasional yells of triumph or frustration came from both teams.

When the winning team was announced, my arms shot up into the air. Leif's team had won the tag competition. The older boys lifted him up on their shoulders. They all were given a medal which they wore around their necks attached to a ribbon, like they were in the Olympics, though these medals were cheap and had Hackley Youth Center and #1 stamped on them.

Even Sir Ballard, though he didn't smile, looked lighter—pleased with his teammates.

"My baby needs prayer and water," said Grandma Eleanor. "Did you see him?" She was more excited than the majority of the parents and family members who attended. Although, she had warned us that she would be. "My little Leif was moving so fast that he about pushed his soul out of his body!" She cackled at her joke. "Look at his walk. He's got a little bounce to it. He's feeling confident. Look at him."

Leif held his head high as he strutted over.

"Aren't you excited, Alaina? What's wrong with you?" asked Grandma Eleanor.

I had been, but it wore off. I think I had a deficiency in endorphins. "I don't know. My condition is undiagnosed. Alainatism," I told her.

"All righty," she responded. "Go and get your friends. I told the team that we would get pizza."

"Did you really? Can I bring a friend too?" I asked.

"This is for the team."

"But I'm going, and I'm not on the team," I said with a brow raised.

"She's got a point," said Leif.

"Hurry up then."

I ran to Alaysia. "Can you go for pizza?"

"I don't know. I'll have to ask my aunt. Can my siblings come too?"

"It's for the team but I asked if you could come."

"I don't know. My mom said we are not supposed to split up and what one does we all do. And I'm in charge while we are out of town and have to follow her rules."

"I totally get it. We don't have enough room in the car, but Anthony is on the team too, so if your aunt can drop all of you off, I suppose it's okay." At least I hoped it was. I mean, I didn't think Grandma Eleanor would turn them away after they were already there.

Alaysia looked relieved. "Okay, see you there."

Next, I ran over to Sir. "Good job," I told him. "We're going for pizza, want to come?"

"Is this because I told you about my food problems at—"

"No, I had forgotten about all that. This is for the team. You can ride with us." I smiled at him and for a brief second, he looked pleasant. "I guess I can."

"I'm glad," I told him. And I meant it. I thought the team camaraderie was good for him.

A boy from the losing team approached and snickered.

"What are you looking at," Sir asked with a sneer.

"I wanted to ask you something."

"Then ask."

He hesitated, but his friend nudged him as if to say, "Go ahead, ask him."

"Why is there a hole in your shoe?" he finally asked.

Who does something like that? I had already noticed Sir trying to hide the hole, but I wouldn't have said anything. I turned to the two boys, smirking like they were so proud of themselves for calling someone out for not having what they did. "Seriously? This is what you do because you lost the game? That's why I'd rather hang out with him," I said, pointing at Sir, "than you. Why are you even here? Did you follow us?"

"Whatever, Nose-bleed," the boy said and walked away with his teammate.

"Let's go," I told Sir. "Do you need to call your mom or dad and tell them you're going with us?" I asked on the way to the car.

He shook his head, and I didn't question him about it.

The car ride over was weird. In the backseat were Leif, Sir, and Patrick. The weird part was Grandma Eleanor kept glancing in her rearview mirror at them. But I couldn't figure out why. Maybe she could feel the simmering anger in Sir that I usually felt, that somehow had lessened today. Whatever the reason, she was quieter than usual. Much quieter than she had been at the game.

We arrived at the restaurant and hurried inside out of the cold. The other cars arrived right behind us. I think the team was going to make the restaurant sorry we ever came in, and I hoped Grandma Eleanor was going to tip our servers well. She was part of the problem though, celebrating just as loudly as they were. There were fifteen of us, three tables, and three pizzas on each table.

This was an old school pizzeria with vintage red and white checkered tablecloths and classic black and white photos of Italy hanging on the walls. It was next door to an arcade, but the wall connecting them was removed so that you could walk right from one to the other. When we finished eating, some of the team went over there.

"Sir," I said, walking over and sitting in the empty seat beside him. "You've been going to the center for a while. Do you know a kid named Deuce?"

His eyes widened. "Why are you asking about him?"

"I heard he's autistic."

"Yeah, and . . .?"

"I haven't seen him in a while," I lied. "I'm just concerned."

Sir's face softened. "I haven't seen him either."

Patrick scooted his chair up so that we had to move our chairs over to make room for him coming in between us. "What are you guys talking about over here? You know what I heard? Somebody said that you dropkicked a dude once," he told Sir.

"Who said it?"

"I just told you, I heard about it."

Sir tossed his napkin on the table. "That was a wrestling move I was practicing for the team. I didn't just randomly dropkick someone."

"Thanks for clearing that up, Bro. So, Alaina... How about some Skee-Ball?"

"Why? Because I'm a girl? Do you think that's all we play?"

"No, I—"

"Okay, stop your begging. I'll school you in Skee-Ball."

"School me? Oh, it's on," Patrick replied with a laugh.

"Grandma," I yelled and pointed into the next room so she would know where I was. She nodded and continued talking with Alaysia's Aunt.

Sir never joined everyone in the arcade. When asked why, he simply said, "That's not real life." He sat watching us from the other room for a while. Shortly after that, he left the pizzeria.

I ran outside and chased him down the sidewalk. "Sir! Sir! I know you hear me!" He stopped walking. "Are you okay?" I asked.

"What are you, everybody's savior?"

"Can you not have that attitude with me? You may not be used to people caring, but I do."

"I'm fine."

"Are you sure? You seem . . . troubled." I pressed gently, hoping he would let down that wall that sprang up whenever absolutely anyone tried to talk to him.

Sir hesitated for a moment before letting out a long sigh. "It's just . . . things haven't been easy for me lately," he admitted.

"You'll be okay. You're strong." I clasped his hand for a second and drew back with a gasp. "What was that?"

"What was what?"

"What did I just feel?"

CHAPTER TWENTY-ONE

S ir's brows rose. "Static electricity?"

"No..."

The moment our skin touched, a jolt of icy shock rippled through me, like I'd grabbed a live wire.

I stared at my hand, still tingling from the strange sensation. Sir shifted uncomfortably, shoving his hands in his pockets. "It was nothing," he muttered. "Just static, like I said."

Maybe he was right. Whatever it was, I didn't like it.

"What's really wrong with you-the reason you're leaving. Are you ill, is that it?"

Sir's face darkened, his eyes flashing with anger for a brief moment before he composed himself.

"Nothing's wrong with me," he said evenly. "You're not a healer gleamer. And I don't know what kind of gleamer you are or what you thought you felt, but I can assure you I'm perfectly fine."

Yet as he spoke, I noticed a strange shadow pass over his features; there one moment and gone the next. I shook my head. *I'm seeing things. That was from a passing car.*

"I'm sorry, I shouldn't have pressed." I mumbled. I rubbed my hands over my arms. "I can be pushy sometimes. It's just . . . Is something wrong?"

Sir shrugged, already turning away. "Don't go looking for problems that aren't there."

Well excuse me! I exclaimed inside.

With that, he walked off down the sidewalk, hands shoved in his pockets, shoulders hunched against the cold. Something wasn't right with Sir. Even when he was trying to be nice, something made alert sirens go off inside my head whenever I was near him.

"Here's your coat," said Alaysia when I went back inside. "I know you're freezing." She looked out the window and down the street. "There's something seriously wrong with that boy."

"You think so too, huh?"

Across the room Grandma Eleanor's eyes met mine. And though she had been smiling at a parent in conversation, her eyes weren't smiling at all.

She didn't question me about Sir or what was going on. She didn't even bring up me following him. I expected her to go into parent mode on the way home, telling me I wasn't thinking and shouldn't have gone out there alone, without telling her, and adding that someone could have kidnapped me. But she was quiet and Leif was also—full after eating half a pizza and sure to have a good night's sleep.

"Is Deuce still at our house?" I asked Grandma Eleanor as she pulled into the garage.

"I don't know what you mean."

"The boy. Deuce. The one who was here last night..."

"I have no idea what you are talking about," she said and went inside the house, leaving the door open behind her.

The next day at the youth center, Alaysia ran up to me and pulled me to the side. "Alaina, last night, after we left the pizza shop, you won't believe what I saw. I was like, *what?* I mean, I screamed, and she said, 'What?' and I said, 'Back up, back up!' It was between two buildings."

"Wait, slow down. You're not making sense. *She* who?"

"Selah."

"Okay, what did you see?"

"Did you know there's a mural of Sheena Meyer downtown in an alley? I looked it up online. It was in the news. They're removing it because it was illegally done. Some random person put it up there. The reporter was all, "I wonder who she is?' But I recognized her."

"Alaysia, Do you think you can show me where it is?"

"Absolutely!"

"Good, because I want to see it."

"You think it has something to do with our mission? Is that why you took her coat? Ooo, I think I've figured it out. So they will think you are her and we can capture them?"

"We?"

"We're the A-team. You need my help."

"How could I possibly look like her? I'm darker than she is. She's like my mom's coffee with cream and I'm like my grandmother's espresso with a drop of oat milk."

Alaysia laughed at me, but I didn't know I was being funny. I was serious.

"What's so funny," asked Selah, walking up to us.

"She thinks she looks like espresso with a drop of oat milk."

Selah laughed and I did too. I didn't realize how it sounded until I heard her say it.

At lunch, Alaysia pulled me aside. "I've been thinking about how this can work. You know, going to see the mural."

"Okay, I'm listening."

"Christmas Eve."

"But—"

"Hear me out. It's the only way to get us all downtown. We can all go there for the festivities."

"But that's also the night of the play they're putting on here."

"So we can go there first," she suggested.

I slowly nodded. The problem was, I was supposed to handle this mission by Christmas day. That meant I had until midnight that night. All I knew was that the mural had better amount to something substantial that could help me.

As we made our way back to our table, Selah asked what we were talking about.

"We were just discussing plans for Christmas Eve," Alaysia answered smoothly.

"Oh yeah? What are your plans?"

"We want to go downtown and check out the holiday lights and everything," Alaysia replied, glancing at me.

"I didn't know you were interested in that kind of thing," Selah commented skeptically.

"I am now," I replied with a smile. "I'm feeling festive."

Selah seemed satisfied with my response and dropped the subject.

The rest of the day passed by quickly and before I knew it, it was time for the rehearsal for the play. I wasn't in it. Acting was not my thing. If they wanted me to hold up a sign or something, that would be more fitting. So I helped with the props.

I used a blade to carve out Styrofoam angels and traced out the detail on them with a marker.

Patrick practiced his role as a lost boy who eventually finds his way home, capturing the heart of the Christmas play. Meanwhile, an adult would operate a smoke machine to set the mood as Sir entered the scene, symbolizing an evil presence that would be transformed by the spirit of Christmas.

Alaysia was good at sewing and helped with the costumes. Others practiced their lines with each other. Musicians from a local church also came in to help and I had to keep an eye on Leif, pulling him away from their guitars.

Afterward, Alaysia reminded me about our plans for Christmas Eve. "I'll text you the best place to meet up."

I nodded. Christmas Eve. It was cutting it so close. *I don't know how I'm supposed to do this.*

Chapter Twenty-Two

Christmas Eve was in two days, and I still had no idea how I was going to help Sheena Meyer. Yeah, I had her coat. Okay, it did lead me to Mr. Tobias, but what now? *'Some gleamer'*, I thought, repeating Sir's words. The fate of the entire town rested on my shoulders.

I paced back and forth in my bedroom. For a moment, I considered marching right down to the library and demanding the gleaming book tell in detail what I needed to do. But all I could think was, *it's going to pile more onto what my thirteen-year-old brain is already trying to handle*, adding to my overwhelming jumble of thoughts. *Nope.*

My phone kept buzzing with calls from my best friend, Penelope. But I didn't want to talk about shopping and boys and stuff. This was a life-or-death situation. The pressure of it all caused a knot in my stomach and I laid down on my bed on my side, hugging myself, trying to calm my nerves.

I closed my eyes, tears welling up. "Heaven . . . please . . . " I whispered. "I just need a little help."

Somehow, I drifted off to sleep. When I opened my eyes, I saw someone standing over me. My fist shot up and met the side of his face.

"Oww!" he screamed and started crying.

"Deuce? What are you doing here? Why are you in my room?"

Deuce stumbled back, holding a hand to his cheek, as Grandma Eleanor burst into the room. I saw the shock on her face at seeing him. Her floral robe swished around her as she hurried to his side. "What happened?" she demanded, looking between us.

Deuce's voice trembled as he spoke, his lip already starting to swell. "She punched me in the face," Deuce cried.

"Alaina!"

"No, that's not what happened. I awoke and he was standing over me."

I jumped out of bed, my heart pounding like it might explode. It all happened so fast, and I didn't trust him—at all. "Deuce, why were you standing over me while I slept?"

Deuce sniffled, still holding his jaw where I had struck him. "I'm sorry," he mumbled. "I didn't mean to scare you. I just ... I wanted to see if you were okay."

"Why would I not be okay?" It didn't make sense. He was lying. I was certain of it.

"That was very inappropriate, Deuce. You should never enter a girl's room without permission, especially at night. Alaina had every right to defend herself."

Deuce hung his head. "I know, I'm really sorry. I wasn't thinking. I just wanted to talk to you about something important."

I studied Deuce curiously. *What could be so urgent that he snuck into my room in the middle of the night?*

"Okay, what did you want to talk to me about?"

Deuce glanced nervously at Grandma Eleanor. "I needed to warn you about . . . the thing."

I studied Deuce's slumped form. His face was blotchy from crying. As annoyed and freaked-out as I was, I felt bad for hitting him.

Grandma Eleanor took him by the shoulders, "Let's get you back to your room."

Mintz appeared out of nowhere and took him by the hand. And for a moment, I thought I saw a slight grin because I remembered to punch rather than scream.

Grandma Eleanor sat on the edge of my bed. "Are you okay?"

"Yes. So, Grandma, Shiloh is a safe place for kids like Deuce?"

"And adults."

"How long do they stay here?"

"Until we can get them to safety."

"Safety from whom?"

"Don't ask questions you already know the answers to."

I thought of my next question but didn't ask it because I realized he must be a gleamer. "Deuce seems worried about me. He must have a reason to be. He knows something. Where is he staying here that we haven't seen him?"

"Hmmm . . . good questions," she replied and left the room.

A day passed with no sign of Deuce. The next day was Christmas Eve. Packages arrived from our parents, the house smelled of delicious holiday foods, and everyone was cheerful, but it didn't feel real. I couldn't explain it, but it was like a disguise over the real thing. Sir had said something similar at the pizzeria.

When no one was around, I wandered into the living room and found Leif's feet sticking from under the Christmas tree. "What are you doing?" I asked.

"Looking for Deuce."

"Get out from under there before Grandma Eleanor sees you." I had to admit, I was curious about if he was still in the house also. "I've got an idea. If he's here, I bet we can find him. Let's look for him."

Leif backed from under the tree with tinsel snagged in his hair. "Like a real search and rescue?"

"Yeah . . . okay."

We searched in every room on every floor for Deuce but never found him. "I guess he went home," I told Leif, seeing his disappointment. He really wanted to find something.

Later that afternoon, Mintz drove us downtown. We found a parking space and she took Leif's hand and walked us over to the choir that was singing. That's where Alaysia texted me to meet her.

The choir members wore matching scarlet robes, their smiles wide as they sang in harmony. On either side of them stood giant fake gingerbread houses. People shuffled in every direction, pausing to take in the sights and listen to the music.

Mintz tucked her scarf inside of her coat. "We really could have done something indoors, you know?"

"Yeah, but this feels like *A Christmas Carol*."

"Code red, we've got a movie buff on our hands," she replied without the slightest hint of a grin.

"So not funny," I said and waved my hand high over my head. "Alaysia!"

She jogged over to me.

"You made it. Where's your family?" I asked.

"Over there," she pointed and turned to the choir. "It's too cold out here for singing. They should have used a recording or something."

"Mintz, we'll be right back," I said. She pointed at her eyes and then at me. I nodded. *She's so dramatic. I know she's really a secret agent.*

I wore Sheena's coat, walking through the crowd of holiday shoppers. Alaina led me past some shops, to an alley.

"Ta-daaaa!" she said, lifting her hand toward the brick wall.

I looked up at the mural. A string of lights hung over it connected to the next building. I had only seen Sheena Meyer once, but this really was her, and the artist had serious skills. "Look at this thing—the detail."

"Didn't I tell you?" asked Alaysia.

"It's totally her." The artist had painted the mural in shades of red, white, and black.

There was a break in the music, and I looked behind us, hearing a commotion of laughter. *Is that Chana?* Some people passed behind us and through them I saw her white coat with the furry hood pulled over her hair. *Who is she with?* She moved to the left just enough for me to see . . . "Oh, no. She's here."

"Who?"

"Sheena Meyer."

Alaysia followed my eyes.

"Let's go and say hello. Should we?"

"Are you crazy? I'm wearing her coat. I'll look like some kind of weird kid stalker."

"Oh, yeah, right."

"Let me think a moment." This was the last day of my mission. If someone wanted to get Sheena, she was right there in the open, holding a giant candy cane. *Why does she have to be here?*

I turned away from Alaysia, pretending to look around. "Chana," I whispered. "Get her out of here." I don't know how, but I knew she could hear me—at least I believed she could. When I turned around, they were gone.

I pulled the coat tightly around me and lifted the hood over my head. My braid-out made my hair crinklier and the locks swung in the wind. "Do I look like her?" I asked Alaysia.

"Who, Sheena? Actually you do. Except that you are espresso with a shot of oat milk."

I started to smile, but my attention went to a man standing atop a narrow, snow-dusted staircase clinging to the side of the building across from the mural. His silhouette dark and still against the twinkling backdrop of the Christmas lights and cheerful crowd. He wore a long black coat and a cap pulled low over his eyes, he scanned the bustling street. Something about him was out of place—like if the scene were a drawing and you erased him, you would say, "Now it's perfect." He was throwing the whole thing off.

Maybe he was just searching for someone, trying to spot his wife in the sea of shoppers or waiting for a friend running late, but the way he kept shifting on the steps, glancing over his shoulder now and then, had an urgency about it.

"Come on, let's get going. We have to get to the play," I told Alaysia, and hurried away from the alley.

"Sheena! Sheena Meyer!" someone called—a boy's voice.

I glanced over my shoulder. The man's head snapped in my direction. I quickly turned away and picked up my pace, aware that, even if he couldn't see my face, with my hair hanging from the hood of her coat, I looked just like her.

He's after Sheena!

Chapter Twenty-Three

"Yo, don't act like you don't know me!" the boy yelled.

"Hurry," I told Alaysia as we pushed through the crowd, my heart pounding.

"Why are we running? Who is that boy? She looked over her shoulder. "Ooo, I think that's Cameron. He's cute, right? I remembered his name from one of my past visits. He attended the youth center summer program before.

I pulled her closer. "That man back there—I think he's chasing us."

Alaysia looked behind us and pulled away from me.

"Hey!"

She jumped up and down waving her hands in the air.

"What are you doing?" *Is she waving at the man?*

People around us were singing along with the song that played from the speakers, "Just hear those sleigh bells . . ."

"I see him. Keep going, Alaina."

"Don't you run from me, girl!" Cameron exclaimed, jokingly.

If I'm Sheena, and I'm ignoring him, why won't he just let me go?

As I stepped around a woman carrying three red bags and a boxed cake, I glanced behind me. The man was now weaving his way through the throng, shoving past clusters of laughing groups and couples, his movements urgent and deliberate, like a predator closing in on its prey. But Cameron beat him to us, bounding in with the grace of an athlete. "Hey," he said, his voice light but edged with curiosity as he jumped in front of me, blocking my way back to Mintz and Leif. He gave a playful laugh. "Who are you running from?"

I kept my head down.

"I must be getting taller because I know you're not shrinking."

Immediately, the guy was right beside Cameron. I looked down at two pairs of feet: Timberlands and a pair of worn construction-looking boots.

I raised my head.

"Oh, you're not Sheena," said Cameron. "I'm sorry. I thought you were."

"No, I'm not." I looked at the guy. Now he wore a ski mask under his cap, and even with that covering most of his face, his anger showed in his eyes. He looked around over my head, and I worried if Chana had gotten Sheena far enough away yet. "But I'm just as important."

The guy stopped looking around and his head lowered like he was looking at me over glasses. I don't think I had ever seen anyone look so evil through a mask. On television yes, but not in real life.

"Look at his fingers," whispered Alaysia. The tips were covered in red and black paint, removing any doubt I had that he had painted the mural.

The man stepped closer to me as if he were going to snatch me away right then and there, in front of everyone.

Cameron's arm shot out in front of him. "Wait, do you know this guy? I don't like how you're looking at this little girl. She's only eleven. Where's your mother."

"I'm thirteen."

"Corey, Theodore," he shouted.

The guy turned to run. At the same time, he grabbed my hand and pulled me along with him.

"Hey!" yelled Alaysia and grabbed my free hand.

The man stumbled forward, losing his footing, and fell, taking us and some other people down with him. I quickly rolled to the side, narrowly avoiding his outstretched arms. Before I could react, Cameron and Alaysia were by my side, pulling me up. It all happened so fast that I wasn't sure how he fell. Then I saw them. While the man was focused on barreling through the crowd, Anthony and Sahara had subtly moved into his path, dropping to their knees just in time to catch his legs. *That's why she jumped and waved her hands. She signaled for their help.*

"Alaysia—"

"In this business, you must have backup," she said with a grin. "We're a team, remember? Plus, that's what the dwarfs did in Stephen Woodruff's book."

"Are you good?" asked Cameron.

"I am."

Theodore, and I guessed the older boy was Corey, ran over. "Hey, isn't that Sheena's coat?" asked Theodore.

Cameron nudged him. "You think the store only made one coat?"

"Of course not, but that tear on the pocket—I remember when she punched me for snagging it."

I grasped it. "He's gone. You guys are awesome. Thank you."

"There are officers over there. Stay near them, okay?" said Cameron.

"Will do."

They watched us walk away. "That girl tried to tell me she's thirteen. She's not a day over eleven."

I heard Cameron but ignored the comment. I was used to it. "You guys get to your aunt," I told Alaysia. "I'll see you at the play."

"Are you sure you're safe?"

I looked around us, not seeing the man anywhere. "Yes," I said and hurried to where I was supposed to meet Mintz and Leif.

"The plan is we stop at home, pick up your grandmother, and head to the youth center for the play," said Mintz.

"She's going to love it," Leif replied, going on and on about his duties in the play as we drove.

All the while, I kept thinking, *save Sheena by midnight*. But wasn't that what I had just done? She got away. Was it over?

The house was totally dark when we pulled up the driveway. At the front door, Mintz tried her keys, but they didn't work. "What happened to the lock?" she thought aloud.

We banged on the door. "Grandma, it's us. Open the door."

But there was no response, and her SUV was right there in the driveway.

Mintz pulled out her phone and tried to call her, but she didn't pick up. "I'm going around to the other side of the house," said Mintz. "Stay here."

The world hushed as we waited. For some reason I didn't feel the cold. I looked down at Leif's wide, worried eyes and took his hand.

Suddenly, the door unlocked and creaked open.

We glanced at each other.

"Was it stuck or something?"

"I don't know," I replied softly.

"Are we going in?" asked Leif.

Instead of answering him, I entered the house cautiously with Leif behind me, my eyes struggling to adjust to the darkness. Every curtain was drawn and every blind closed. I had never known Grandma Eleanor to close anything but her bedroom curtains at night.

A heaviness hung in the air and lowered, weighing down on me. "Grandma?" I called.

I gripped Leif's hand tighter, feeling his small fingers clench mine in return.

We moved slowly from the foyer and through the front hall. "Mintz?" I called.

Leif's breath quickened as we reached the base of the staircase. "Maybe Grandma is sleeping?" His small voice held a desperate hope.

I nodded, though when did she ever sleep this early in the evening? Plus, she knew we were going to the play, and she wouldn't miss that for anything.

We climbed the stairs, and the air grew heavier with each step.

At the top, I froze. Ten feet away, Grandma Eleanor lay motionless on the floor.

CHAPTER TWENTY-FOUR

I held up the light from my phone. From the darkest corner of the landing, a swirling black mass writhed and billowed, seeming to grow larger by the second.

I stepped in front of Leif, trying to shield him from seeing our grandmother's limp body on the floor. But he saw her anyway and broke free from my grasp, running to her side. "Grandma!" he cried.

I knelt beside her. Not looking away from the corner of the room. My hand moved down from her head to her neck. Her body was still warm. And there was a pulse.

"She's alive," I said.

Suddenly Leif looked up. "What is that?"

"The Murk," I whispered and stood, still unable to tear my eyes from it.

How was it here? We were safe at Shiloh. Grandma Eleanor said so herself. We, and others, were always safe here. *How did it get in?* I thought of the man downtown who wanted Sheena Meyer. Could it have been him? He would have had to figure out who I was, our address, and then beat us here. The only real thing that made sense was that someone brought it in. Someone like . . . Deuce. He was disguised as someone we could trust. That was the only answer.

"Stand up, Leif." I told him.

"But Grandma—"

"Stand up!" I shouted. "She's going to be okay."

The front door slammed shut downstairs. Leif hurried to my side and grabbed my hand. Then I noticed movement at the other end of the hall at the back stairwell.

"Leif, how fast can you run?"

"Huh?"

I lowered my voice. "Run to Mintz, Leif."

He stood frozen.

"Leif . . . Tag!"

He shot off and slid under the Murk and right past it. Mintz caught him on the other end. "Get him out of here!" I yelled.

They disappeared down the back stairs.

I faced the swirling darkness. It loomed larger, spreading through the walls and doors.

"Alaina, hurry!" Mintz yelled from the bottom of the stairs.

I glanced back at Grandma Eleanor. Her chest rose and fell slightly. She was alive, but weak. The Murk loomed closer. Whatever this thing had done to her, somehow, I had to make sure it didn't finish the job.

"Get away from her!" I shouted, my voice trembling. "How dare you come to Shiloh. This is a place of peace and love and

... and ... of God. You don't belong here," I said, trying to sound braver than I felt. "Go back to wherever you came from and leave my family alone!"

It swirled faster, lashing out a smoky tendril toward me. I dove over it.

"Alaina, what are you doing? Run!" Grandma Eleanor's weak voice said from behind me.

I glanced back. "I can't leave you here, Grandma."

"My brave girl. Go. Save your brother. I love you."

I hesitated, with tears in my eyes, before sprinting after Leif. The shadowy mass swelled towards me, tendrils grasping. I ducked and wove, Grandma's warnings echoing in my mind: the Murk feeds on fear.

"I love you!" I yelled, and drawing on every ounce of courage, I burst through the writhing darkness. It clung to me like cobwebs, but I broke free and raced down the stairs. Leif and Mintz were now already outside, on the deck at the back of the house.

"There she is!" Mintz exclaimed.

"Alaina!" Leif wrapped his arms around me. "What about Grandma?" he cried.

"She's going to be okay," I said, trying to convince myself as much as him. Looking back at the house, I saw shadows creeping around the windows. The Murk was consuming Shiloh like a plague.

"It's coming, I will hold it off as long as I can." Mintz kissed the top of both of our heads, and I was too far into flight mode to be shocked at her showing some type of affection. "Go!" she screamed.

We ran and I didn't know where we were going, but a glint of light flashed by, just like in my dream, and I followed it.

"Look, Leif!" I couldn't believe my eyes. Two snowmobiles were tucked beneath a tarp behind the greenhouse. "Why didn't Grandma tell us she had snowmobiles?" And there were helmets out there too?

My heart raced as I yanked off the tarp and swung a leg over the snowmobile's seat, gripping the cold handlebars. My fingers fumbled momentarily, but muscle memory from the safety course my dad made me take kicked in.

"Get on, Leif!" I yelled. We put on the helmets, and I flipped the ignition switch and pulled the starter cord hard. The engine sputtered, the vibrations buzzing through my arms as the machine came alive beneath me. Leif clambered on behind me, wrapping his arms tightly around my waist.

We shot across Grandmother Eleanor's property, and I could hear Leif in my head. I knew my brother. *Do you know where you're going?"*

I knew the general direction. And then there was that glint that I kept seeing. The same one I saw outside of my bedroom window the night before we left home to come to Michigan. I saw it in the trees ahead. Guiding me. I drove alongside the trees in the clearing. There was no way I was going to try to maneuver between them.

The snowmobile's headlights cut twin beams through the inky darkness as I gunned the throttle. The wind whipped against my helmet. I leaned forward, seeing a vast sheet of ice ahead—the Muskegon River. And beyond it, the holiday light-covered homes of people ignorant of the evils of the world. My breath caught as we shot forward—down the hill and right over the frozen surface. Light snow sprayed out from beneath us in a glittering arc, and I hoped the ice was thick enough to hold us.

Every second felt like a race against the unseen—sharp turns around hidden snowdrifts, patches of rough ice that made the snowmobile jolt and shudder beneath us. I kept my eyes locked ahead. My brother clung to my waist, his grip firm.

"We're riding for too long. We're going to need gas," I knew Leif would say next. And I would explain that we could go about 100 miles on a tank of gas, and that our grandmother's house wasn't nearly far enough away from society to use that much up.

As I reached the far side of the river, my eyes darted frantically, searching for any spot where the bank wasn't a wall of ice and snow. The shoreline was uneven, with jagged chunks of frozen debris piled high, but up ahead, I spotted a narrow gap leading into a sloping backyard. It was our only chance. I veered sharply, guiding the snowmobile toward the opening, the tracks churning up loose snow as we powered up the incline. We barreled past an old wooden fence, skimming close to a line of bare, skeletal trees, and tore through the backyard of someone's property—a stretch of snow-covered grass littered with lawn chairs. We navigated the maze of obstacles, cutting a path back to solid ground.

Suddenly, Leif's hands dug into me.

Something's wrong. Is someone behind us? Then I remembered the other snowmobile. *If that's what it is, who's on it? Mintz, coming to rescue us?*

We ducked, hearing an explosion from across the river. *Was that Grandma Eleanor's house?*

Chapter Twenty-Five

Grandma Eleanor... I wanted to cry, but I refused to. I couldn't... yet. Not until I was certain.

There was no time to stop. Especially with someone following us. And I knew she wouldn't want me to. I didn't even know where the police station was, not that they would believe anything I told them. And I didn't know the rules for driving a snowmobile through town. It was a good thing Muskegon was a maze of alleys through neighborhoods. That was the best way to travel, and they would not have been plowed like the roads, so I headed down to the nearest one.

Again, I knew what Leif was thinking. *Do you know where you're going?*

"Not exactly," I would have responded, meaning not at all, but then we came from an alley between fenced backyards, and I realized the building down the street was Nelson School.

If we were near Nelson, then we were also near Mr. Tobias's house and not far from the youth center. I looked left and right and shot off.

At the last minute, I glimpsed a sign: Monroe Street. I took a hard right, the snowmobile fishtailing on the icy road.

I pulled right up the driveway and into the backyard of Mr. Tobias's little white house, barely missing the steps on the side, and brought the snowmobile to a skidding stop.

Leif and I leaped off, threw our helmets onto the ground and ran for the side door. I pounded urgently on the wood, praying Mr. Tobias was home.

"Mr. Tobias!" I shouted. "Please, you have to help us!"

After what seemed like an eternity, the door creaked open. Mr. Tobias peered out, his face creased in concern. "Children! What's happened?" Behind his glasses, his eyes were wide with alarm. Before he could speak, the roar of an approaching engine cut through the icy air.

He looked above our heads at the trees on the other side of the driveway. In that instance it was as if Mr. Tobias knew . . . everything.

"There's no time, we have to get to the youth center right away!"

I gasped. "The youth center? The Christmas play is tonight. Is there help there?"

Mr. Tobias backed up his wheelchair and stood.

"Y-you can walk?"

"He held a finger to his lips as if to say, "Don't tell anyone," grabbed his coat and ushered us back outside. "I'll drive. Quickly now! Come on, boy!" he said and hurried down the steps and to the garage. He unlocked the side door and went inside.

I took Leif's hand. "Why did he say, 'Come on, boy?'"

"I don't know. I'm already coming," said Leif.

We turned, hearing someone. Deuce came running out with his coat and shut the door behind him. "I'm coming. Let's do this, Mr. Tobias!"

"Is that Deuce?" Leif asked.

"That kid is everywhere."

Leif and I glanced at each other and then followed them.

There was a truck in the garage, and it wasn't tiny. No wonder the garage was so large. I thought we would need a ladder to climb inside. Mr. Tobias was agile and climbed right in. I helped Leif up and then I climbed in.

As the garage door rose, I saw the lights of the other snowmobile, from down the street.

"Someone followed us."

"Don't worry. They won't come here."

"But we thought the same about Grandma Eleanor's house."

He stared at me. His expression softened for a moment. "Yeah, well . . . This is different."

And just like he said, the snowmobile that had followed and somehow found us, rode away and the lights disappeared.

"Who was that?" asked Leif.

"My guess would be ... Luke. Trust me, he won't be far." Mr. Tobias held up a hand towards me. "I know you have questions, Alaina. And I promise you will get answers soon. But right now, we need to focus on getting you and your brother someplace safe."

Good. That's good. I thought. I've never wanted my parents so badly before in my life. I wanted to scream for them, like when I was a kid, until they appeared. That safety and protection we had always felt with them was gone. I glanced at Leif. I had to be that for him.

The truck rumbled down the snowy streets, its massive tires crunching over the ice. I looked in the side-view mirror to see if the other snowmobile followed us, and then out the window, watching the cozy homes of the neighborhood: the colored lights and inflated snowmen beginning to deflate, Christmas trees sparkling inside of windows. All of these people, safe in their homes, not knowing anything about the Murk.

Leif huddled close to me

Mr. Tobias's gaze fixed intently on the road ahead.

It wasn't long before he pulled the truck into the parking lot of the Hackley Youth Center. It was full of vehicles.

"This is someplace safe?" I asked.

"This is where it happens."

"Where what happens?"

"Quickly now, inside," he urged.

"Without you? Are you sure?"

"Certain," Tobias replied.

My legs wobbled a bit as I hopped out and then helped Leif climb down from the truck, while scanning the groups walking toward the community center. Without looking back or even getting a goodbye from Mr. Tobias, we walked toward the building. Deuce trailed behind, his head swiveling all around as if on high alert, humming.

I had heard the melody before. Then he got a little louder. "I'm a soldier in the army of the Lord . . ."

"Seriously, Deuce?"

"What?"

Leif tugged at me. "Why did we come here? What about Grandma and Mintz?" he asked, his eyes watering.

"They're okay. I know they are." I lied, but it made me feel better to try to be positive for him.

A familiar face stood out through the glass of the front entrance—Alaysia, holding a program and peering around anxiously.

We hurried to the building, and the front doors swung open, letting out a rush of warm air and bright fluorescent lights. I blinked, adjusting to the change from outside.

"Alaina! You're here!" yelled Alaysia. "What took you so long? Her face fell as she took in my disheveled appearance and the look on my face. "What happened? Are you okay?"

"You look like you got dragged through a snowdrift!" said her sister, Sahara.

"Don't you have a filter? Not now," said Alaysia. She took us off to the side.

My mouth opened, but no words came out. For the first time that evening, the reality of the last few hours suddenly crashed down on me. My composure was starting to crack, tears welling up in my eyes.

Alaysia immediately wrapped me in a hug. "I knew we shouldn't have split up. I mean, haven't movies taught us that?"

"Alaysia, I've failed."

"No, you haven't. Don't even set your mouth to say those words—my mom says that. But my mom is right, don't say it. You haven't failed. Sheena Meyer is safe."

"But you don't know what happened."

"I don't care what happened. Don't give up hope, Alaina. It's okay, you're safe now," she said gently. I clung to my friend, desperately trying to regain control of my emotions.

"Okay." I sniffed and dried my eyes. "Okay," I said again.

"Why is Deuce with you?"

"Your guess is as good as mine."

The lobby was brightly decorated with lights and the wreaths we made during our craft session. The sound of Christmas carols echoed down the hall.

"Should we go inside to see the production? It has already started," asked Alaina.

I didn't want to watch a play or production or whatever it was. *Why did Mr. Tobias bring us here?* It didn't make sense to me.

I looked outside through the glass doors and his truck was gone. "He really left us."

"Who?" asked Alaysia.

Suddenly I hopped back, pulling her and Leif at the same time. "Oh no . . . "

"What? What happened?"

"She's here?"

"Who's here?"

"Sheena Meyer."

CHAPTER TWENTY-SIX

I backed up. Alaysia pulled Sahara beside her, blocking me off, and we watched Sheena, Chana, and Theodore enter, and pass by in the hall.

I was still stooping when Leif asked, "Why are you doing that?"

"This is where it happens," I said as I stood, repeating Mr. Tobias's words.

Alaysia turned to me with her mouth open. "Okay, what are we doing?"

"I don't know."

"The first thing you need to do is take her coat off," she said, pulling it away from me. "Sahara, put this in the lost and found."

"Got it," she said and ran off with the coat.

I looked up and down the hall. Faking a smile at people saying hello in passing.

"What don't I know?" Alaysia asked.

"Huh?"

"Your team can't help you properly if they don't know what's going on."

I swallowed. "Remember what happened? Something pulling us? That was real and it wants Sheena Meyer. I think it's coming here tonight."

"With all these people? On Christmas Eve?" Her eyes were wide, and her voice was getting more high-pitched with each word. "What are we going to do?"

I shook my head and looked down the hall. "Sir!"

"Yeah, call on the mean boy right now. That's a great idea."

He walked toward the entrance to the basement. I took Leif's hand. Deuce waited. "Oh come on," I said and took his hand too. He grinned, and we ran down the hall. "Sir!" I called, with every male in the vicinity looking at me. "Sorry, not you. Nope, not you either. That's actually his name." *Why couldn't his mother have named him something else.*

"Sir!" I called again following him into a room. He stopped walking. "I know you know what I am. And I think you can help me."

"What you are?" asked Alaysia, behind me.

Sir kept his back to us. "I can't help you. I'm not on your side. Or your team."

"But you've been nice to me."

"I slipped—" He turned around and faced us. "Deuce!"

Deuce let go of my hand and ran to him. Sir knelt and they hugged tightly.

He wiped his eyes. "Why do you have my brother?"

His brother? I remembered Grandma Eleanor's words. Shiloh was a place to keep gleamers safe. "Protecting him. Keeping him safe."

"I thought Mom took you and left," Sir told him. "She's gone."

"They kept me," said Deuce. "Now I'm ready for battle."

"No," said Sir. "You don't understand. You're too young."

"I understand," said Deuce. "We're good, fighting against evil."

"Oh my god, I messed up," said Sir, grabbing his head.

"What did you do?" I asked, stepping closer.

"He said it would change our lives, so we wouldn't be hungry or need things anymore." He looked at Deuce. "Look at you, you're all cleaned up. Look at your clothes. And you didn't have to—to—"

"To what?" I asked.

"Be a sellout."

"Sir, what did you do?"

"Wait," said Alaysia. "What's happening here?"

He didn't have to say anything really. I knew we were in trouble. "She's here," I told him.

"She's here?" Sir exclaimed. "Are you serious?"

"That's why you're here, isn't it—waiting for her to come in one day, so the Murk could capture her?"

"He's talking about Sheena Meyer?" Alaysia asked and hopped with her fists balled at her sides. "I knew it! It's in the book—"

"Not now," I told her.

"I can fix this," said Sir.

We all reached for each other as the room shook. "I think it's too late."

"No it's not. I'm going out there or it will tear this place apart."

"No, I will," I replied.

"No!" said Alaysia.

"You can't," said Sir.

"I have to."

Leif grabbed my hand. "No, don't go."

"You've been a good little brother . . . but right now, I'm not your sister. I'm your protector, just like Mom and Dad would expect me to be in their absence. Alaysia, you've been a great friend. You understand things. Please understand that I have to do this. You and your siblings can help me by keeping Sheena Meyer inside. If she even looks like she's about to leave, guide her back, and say something like, 'Hey, I think you'd love what they're doing backstage.' Or talk about saving the earth or something. Just keep her inside."

Alaysia nodded.

"Sir, in spite of your anger, I've always liked you—even more than Patrick."

He looked shocked for a moment.

"Can you please look after my brother. And one more thing... Forgive yourself. Thank you. For everything."

Before anyone could protest further, I ran out the side exit doors of the building, my heart pounding in my chest. I skidded to a halt outside, breathless. There it was—towering into the sky, its smokey form looming over me.

You're out here, Alaina. What now? Freeze to death?

I pictured my brother and my friends inside. I failed my grandmother, but I wouldn't fail anyone again.

"Stop!" I yelled.

The Murk continued churning over me, like the plume from a chemical plant fire that I had seen on the news.

"I am a traveler!" I yelled.

CHAPTER TWENTY-SEVEN

The churning paused for a moment.

"So you are," a voice hissed.

It heard me . . .

A twisting smokey tendril extended and hovered above me. "What a special holiday surprise. Approach the shadow."

"I know what you want, but you won't get it. Not today," I said.

The Murk let out a rumble, like an approaching storm. I planted my feet, willing myself to be brave. I thought of my grandmother, of my little brother, who wanted nothing other than to be a kid and looked to me for protection now, and of my new friends, trusting me. It was a heavy load, but it also gave me strength.

How bad could this thing be, it was nothing but smoke and fog. But then I looked around at how it was branching out into the neighborhood. Houses were engulfed in its thick fog, trees were withering and dying as the Murk spread its reach. It was trying to consume the entire city, and possibly, even beyond.

"All will be lost unless you turn over your gift to me."

"Never!" I shouted defiantly. "You've already taken enough from this town. You've taken my grandmother, and I won't let you take anyone else!"

The Murk chuckled, a sound like a bulldozer screeching against a wall. "Very well, then. If you insist on attempting to protect these insignificant mortals, I shall plunge them all into eternal darkness. Prepare to witness their demise, gleamer."

"What do you want with my chrono gleaming abilities?" I asked, trying to buy some time.

The Murk's dark mass swirled, coalescing into a vaguely human-like shape. "Ah, curiosity. An admirable trait, for a human," it hissed. "You see, Dear Gleamer, your gift is quite unique. You can not only see but also control the flow of time itself. Imagine the chaos I could unleash with such abilities at my disposal."

I can? If the Murk got a hold of my gleam, it would be able to undo all the good the gleamers had done, and who knows what else. "Not in a million years!"

The Murk chuckled, a menacing sound that raised goosebumps on my arms. "Time, gleamer, is not something you have much of. Join me, and I'll spare your family, your friends … and this pathetic little town that you gleamers are so attracted to."

The offer was tempting. I could save everyone I cared about with just one simple act of betrayal. But what kind of person would I be then? I would be the same as Sir almost was. But I had learned something valuable: Don't make choices when you're feeling fear or anxiety.

I took a deep cold breath, getting myself ready as I shivered. "No."

"No?"

"You don't guide my steps. Heaven does."

A boy—teenager—walked right out of the Murk with an angry strut.

What? How? Who is he? I suddenly felt like a tiny creature in an uncharted world, hoping the shock and terror didn't show on my face.

"Very well, have it your way, Alaina Thompson. Prepare to face the consequences!"

He grabbed me by the arms, squeezing them in at my sides. The whites of his eyes were red. "Give it to me," he said.

"Yes, give it to him," said the twin girls appearing behind him.

The Murk stopped whatever it was doing to the building and a smokey fog circled around me.

"Never," I replied through clenched teeth. "The gleam is stronger than you are." I didn't flinch or back down. I felt a new kind of strength coursing through me, one that came from knowing that I was fighting for something greater than myself.

I closed my eyes, bracing for the impact. Now would be a good time for a multiverse event with other versions of me showing up to tackle those twins. Whatever the boy was going to do to me, I prayed it would be quick.

"You don't know me very well, I will protect my gift with everything that I have, Shadow."

He looked taken aback for a moment. "Shadow? No. I am Drake."

Drake? What happened to Luke? How many people were working for this thing? "I won't let you hurt anyone else," I told him.

"Oh, really? And what makes you think you can stop me? You're just a little girl, barely old enough to understand the ways of this world."

I gasped for air, the darkness seeping through my very pores, trying to extinguish the light within me. My vision started to blur, my limbs heavy with fatigue as I fought inside while the Murk pried at my mind. *I can't... I can't... keep ... this... up.*

And at that moment I prayed.

For a split second, everything went still—almost as if the darkness hesitated. But then, through the smoke, I saw a glimpse of Sir and Leif. And then I didn't see Leif at all as my eyes watered and I began to choke.

Faintly, I heard singing. "I'm a soldier." *No Deuce!*

Something inside of me shifted. It felt like a warm energy, like a fire burning inside of me, spreading throughout my body. Drake's hands released me, and lightning struck around me parting the smoke.

Then I felt arms around me and I was picked up, but my eyes were burning too much to keep them open for long. "Leave her alone," Sir's voice shouted. "I won't let this happen. And I'd rather die than become part of you."

Slowly, I opened my eyes again and saw a shimmering barrier between me and the Murk. I looked around, trying to find the source.

And in the blink of an eye, Mr. Tobias, Grandma Eleanor, Mintz, and a few older people I'd never seen before were there with an energy emitting from them that made the Murk roar.

Deuce's hands pulsed with light.

The Murk twisted and contorted, shadows splitting off and dissolving, until it was gone.

Sir held me up as I caught my breath. I smiled up at him. He took his coat off and placed it around me.

Leif ran to Grandma Eleanor, and I followed. "Grandma!"

"Grandma, you're okay? I'm so sorry about your house. You lost your prized possessions."

"What are you talking about?"

"The house exploded. You lost your library."

"Alaina, I'm looking right at my most prized possessions."

"You mean us?"

"Of course. And my house is fine. The Murk works in illusions, you need to know that."

"Uh, don't you think that would have been good to know from the start?"

"Don't get smart," she said with a grin and hugged me tight. "I'm so proud of you."

People started leaving the center and going out to their cars.

"Don't worry, they didn't see any of it. That's how it works. And if they did, they won't remember when they wake. Tobias, get that monstrosity of a vehicle out of here so people can get out of their parking spaces." She lowered her voice. "And before someone finds out you can walk."

"I'm so proud of you for completing your mission, Alaina."

"But I don't get it, I really didn't do much for Sheena Meyer."

"Well, if you hadn't been downtown, Luke would have seen her. She wouldn't be here right now getting into that SUV with her father."

I glanced over at them. Chana waved and gave me a thumbs up.

"You didn't realize it, but there was another part of your mission. A very important part." She turned me so that I faced Sir. "You saved him. Your kindness and care kept him from joining the Murk. Go and talk to him."

I noticed Alaysia and her siblings coming out of the building. I stopped. "Grandma, you know everything—things you aren't even around to see. Is my friend Alaysia also a gleamer?"

"Probably."

"Really?"

"Everyone on this earth has a touch of the gleam, some stronger than others. But some have allowed their light to extinguish."

That made me remember the guy looking for Sheena Meyer. "That man, Luke, he got away."

"I wouldn't worry about that. I'm sure the authorities will catch him at some point."

"Alaina," Alaysia yelled and waved. I ran over to her, hoping she wouldn't forget everything we had been through together, the next morning or once she got back home. "Is everything okay?"

"Everything is absolutely okay."

"Then I'll say Merry Christmas now, and you make sure, when you get time, that you call and tell me everything. And I don't care that we live in different states, we're the A-team. I'll be back this summer."

"Me too," I said and hugged her.

Then I went over to Sir. "Here's your coat back."

"No, you hold onto it."

"But you're freezing."

"Get on in this car," Grandma Eleanor yelled. "Them, too."

"I guess you and your brother are going with us to Shiloh, Sir Ballard."

"I've been there before. I just didn't know *you* were there or that Eleanor was your grandmother."

Chapter Twenty-Eight

That night, I slept like I hadn't slept in years. And no one tried to wake me in the morning. Leif didn't even come jumping on my mattress, yelling, "It's Christmas!"

It was almost noon when I put on a robe over my pjs and slippers on my feet and made my way downstairs. Everyone was in the kitchen, including Sir and Deuce.

"There she is," said Grandma Eleanor.

I put my hands up shielding my face.

"What are you doing?"

"Preparing for the snowballs you usually send flying through the air."

"She does that?" asked Deuce.

"Yep," Leif and I said. "Thanks for letting me sleep in."

"You needed it. We haven't even opened gifts yet." She lifted a hand around the kitchen. As you can see, "I went a little overboard with breakfast."

"Sounds about right," I replied and hugged her, glancing over at the pancakes, french toast, bacon, frittata, hashbrowns and a tray of assorted fruits and pastries.

I grabbed a piece of french toast and inched my way over to Mintz who sat at a bar stool sipping coffee. I hugged her and kissed her on the cheek.

"Hey, stop getting mushy."

I grinned and sat at the table, looking out of the window. "The snowmobiles are back?"

"They sure are, and who knew you could ride like that?"

"I did." I looked around at everyone. "So, who wants to start?"

"What?"

"What type of gleamer are you?"

"I'd rather open gifts," said Leif.

"I wasn't even talking to you."

Leif folded his arms. "Oh, well how do you think you got away from the Murk-guy?"

"Deuce. Right Deuce? And Sir. And the others."

"And me," said Leif.

"You?"

The phone rang. "Hey, it's Mom!"

"Leif!" said Grandma Eleanor.

"I know Grandma, gleamers are secrets," he replied.

I was in shock. *How long had Leif known?*

After we got off the phone with our parents, Sir walked over to me. "Alaina, I was wondering if we could start all over."

"I would like that."

"My name is Sir, and that's my real name. I think my mother said it by accident and they put it on my birth certificate or something, and she never changed it. Anyway, I wasn't bitten by a radioactive spider, but I have some abilities and have known about them for about four years. I've been doing my best to raise my brother, mostly alone. Someone at the youth center found out. And since your grandmother is the executive director of the center—"

"You are?" I asked, turning to her.

Sir continued. "She found out about us and that we were gleamers. Recently our mom left and never came back."

"But we think we've found your grandmother," said Grandma Eleanor.

"You have?"

She nodded. "Yes."

She lives in Norton Shores and we'll take you there today.

"Later today, I hope."

"Oh you like it here, now?" Grandma Eleanor said with a smirk.

"I guess so. Now that we're out of that hidden suite."

"What hidden suite?" Leif and I asked in unison.

It snowed the morning we were leaving for the airport. Outside my window, the world looked like it had been dipped in a fresh coating of powdered sugar. Snow blanketed the trees and the rooftops of houses down the road. Smoke curled from chimneys, fading into the soft gray sky. I leaned my head against the window frame, realizing how much I was going to miss Shiloh.

While Leif was preoccupied with whatever he was doing, I took a last walk down the steep stairs, down the hall and around another corner to the library, looking up at the enormous double doors. Again, the door was unlocked and I went inside. The Aetates Papilio was on the table, still glowing. I smiled down at it.

Thanks for your help, I said. Finally understanding that it wasn't magical words but angels that were guiding me.

I opened the book and read, "Alaina entered the library for the last time as she prepared to leave for North Carolina. She would never forget her mission, or those involved, or the things she learned. She became a new person."

As I closed the gleaming book, the last traces of its soft glow faded into the darkness of the room. But the memories of everything that happened lingered, etched into my mind forever and filled with the lessons I learned over winter break about friendship, faith, and angels.

I wonder, I thought, as opened the Aetates Papilio one more time and flipped back to the beginning. There was now a title page:

Gleamers Chronicle: Winter Shadows

By Alaina Marie Thompson.

With a smile, I closed the book again. This was just the start of my story. Summer break was coming, and that meant a whole new adventure. We might be leaving Shiloh behind for now, but I would return as a new Alaina—the Alaina who knows about gleamers and her gift—ready for my next gleamer mission.

Please Leave A Review

Your review means the world to me. I greatly appreciate any kind words. Even one or two sentences go a long way in helping readers discover *Gleamers Chronicle Winter Shadows*.

Thank you in advance.

Don't Miss Out!

Exclusive content, discounts, and giveaways are available only to L. B. Anne's VIP members. Use the link below to sign up.

There is no charge or obligation.

www.lbanne.com/vip-club

ALSO BY L.B. ANNE

The Sheena Meyer Series:
The Girl Who Looked Beyond the Stars
The Girl Who Spoke to the Wind
The Girl Who Captured the Sun
The Girl Who Became a Warrior
City of Gleamers
Secret of Shadow and Light
May Your Vision be True
Fate of the Gleam Keeper
Everfall Series:
Before I Let Go
If I fail
All the Scars (Coming 2025)
Knights of the Gleam Series:
Angel Girl Awakening
Hidden Thorns

Standalones:

Snicker's Wish, A Christmas Story
Five Things About Dragon Flies
Never Really Gone
What the Good Girl Knew

About the Author

L. B. Anne is best known for her Christian middle grade, Sheena Meyer, series about a girl with a special gift and a destiny that can save the world. L. B. Anne lives on the Gulf Coast of Florida with her husband and is a full-time author, coach, and mental health advocate. When she's not inventing new obstacles for her diverse characters to overcome, you can find her reading, playing bass guitar, running on the beach, or downing a mocha iced coffee at a local cafe while dreaming of being your favorite author. Visit L. B. at www.lbanne.com

Instagram: Instagram.com/authorlbanne

Facebook: Facebook.com/authorlbanne

Twitter: twitter.com/authorlbanne

Pinterest: pinterest.com/AuthorLBAnne

www.ingramcontent.com/pod-product-compliance
Lightning Source LLC
Chambersburg PA
CBHW032033310726
48972CB00002B/652